Thistle Downe

A Tale of Trolls & Fairies

bright sky press
HOUSTON, TEXAS

2365 Rice Blvd., Suite 202
Houston, Texas 77005

10   9   8   7   6   5   4   3   2   1

Library of Congress Cataloging-in-Publication Data on file with publisher.

ISBN 978-1-942945-14-7

Editorial Direction: Lucy Herring Chambers
Managing Editor: Lauren Adams
Designer: Marla Y. Garcia
Illustrations: Molly & Gary Whitney

Printed in Canada through Friesens

To all those who can let
their imaginations take them
to magical places
where anything is possible
and love can triumph.

Thistle Downe

A Tale of Trolls & Fairies

MOLLY & GARY WHITNEY

bright sky press

HOUSTON, TEXAS

Table of Contents

Preface

This is an inspiring story of determination and of love. The setting is the mid-19th century in the Orkney Islands of Scotland. It is a fantasy tale of an enchanted island where trolls, fairies, and humans interact without regard to their respective sizes. So suspend reality, give your imagination wings, and enjoy the magic!

From the start of his life in a cave you will follow Tyson, a young and very unusual troll, as he strives to overcome his limitations and make a life for himself in the much greater world.

MBW & GSW

Chapter One

The Cave

Gareth shifted slightly in the damp black mud beneath the bridge, smudging the imprint of his large, misshapen body in the sludge. The bridge was built across a brook running beside the road from Stenness to Kirkwall. He waited under it early each morning, ready to rob or rattle anybody trying to cross it. At noon, his mayhem complete, he would abandon the creek bed and retire to a shady spot for a nap. Gareth was a troll—a frightening, craggy mountain of a creature. Coarse hair—once red but now fading to white-covered his head and neck like thick underbrush. He glared at the world through a constant mist of anger and discontent.

In his distant past, Gareth had lived in a different part of this island. He was one of ten children, five older and four younger than he. Stuck squarely in the middle, he was mostly ignored by everyone. He got little attention from his overburdened parents and stayed in the background because it was hard to get a word in edgewise in that house. His main interest was in finding a way out of there. He did not excel at anything in particular, but he did have a goal. He definitely wanted to get away from home and support himself. As soon as he was old enough he learned from a farrier how to forge iron horseshoes and attach them to horses' hooves. Farriers were in great demand, so he was busy. The work did not require him to spend time talking to people, which was perfectly fine with him, since he much preferred the company of horses.

One Saturday, he was at an outdoor market buying fresh vegetables when the smiling girl behind one of the tables engaged him in conversation. Her name, he learned, was Eva. She was a troll herself, a member of a local farming family. Gareth had few friends and little experience with small talk, but the girl was nice, and soon he was a regular customer. At first he was too shy to approach her directly, but she managed to draw him out. Finally, he got up the courage to ask if he could call on her at the farm where she lived. He soon became a steady visitor, and eventually he felt more comfortable with the girl and her family than he ever had with anybody else in his whole life.

Eva was lively and warm. No one could resist her remarkable smile, and Gareth was happy when he was with her. The world around him, which he had mostly ignored, became vibrant and beautiful when he saw it through the happy filter that was Eva. She was always in motion, her black ringlets dancing. They took long walks together around the island, relishing the warm sun on their faces or surrendering to the winds that swept them along the roads. When cold, slanting rains unexpectedly pelted them or swirling sea mists hid their path, they scurried under stone outcroppings for shelter and laughed with delight, kept warm by the joy of being together. They spent a lot of time with her cheerful, noisy family, so unlike most troll families he had known, and over time Gareth knew that he wanted to have a family like that with Eva. As they came to understand each other's hearts, they knew that they belonged together.

So they happily married, and soon a wee bairn, a child, was on the way. Eva expected to bloom with good health, but that was not what happened. She became more and more tired and pale; her once robust strength faded as the weeks passed. On sunny days she sat on the porch of their modest little cottage wrapped in a rough woolen shawl, hoping to warm the icy chill in her bones. She talked constantly about the expected baby. She was certain it was a boy, and she chose to name him Tyson, which meant "high-spirited." Gareth worried and hoped, but he was helpless as Eva's health continued to decline. He tried to keep her warm; he tried to keep her fed. Alas, this story ended sadly. The baby was born, but Eva did not survive the birth.

Something quite remarkable, however, happened at the moment of her passing. Her smile—which had become increasingly rare but was still radiant—and her capacity for love and kindness passed from her frail body to

Tyson's sturdy one, and his little newborn mouth curved into a tender crescent.

Gareth was at first devastated at his loss, then highly resentful. His heart tightened so painfully he could hardly breathe, and then it simply broke apart. The only creature who had ever cared for him was gone, and he was left with this child who had caused it. What could he do now? How could he take care of a baby? Did he even want to? He remembered Eva's joy over Tyson and her determination to bring him into the world, and he knew he would have to find a way.

So he took the baby along with their few belongings and left their village early one morning, saying goodbye to no one, neither his family nor Eva's. He walked for several days, rummaging for food from gardens and finding water in streams. At night he would slip into the fields and take milk from the cows that belonged to local farmers. With it, he fed the baby as best he could because he felt Eva's memory prodding him to do so.

While looking for food one day, he came upon a large cave very near a stream. He was tired of wandering and decided it was as good a place as any to live, so he put Tyson and their belongings inside. The space was deep and high. There was plenty of room for Gareth and Tyson, as well as for two beds made of rushes and rags and a simple fireplace Gareth built of stones and mud from the brook. A quilt Eva had made served as a curtain at the mouth of the cave to shield them from the outside weather. He had brought some of his and Eva's kitchenware along when they left the village, so he fashioned shelves for the crockery and a table out of slabs of rock.

Then, Gareth started to think about what he would do next. He spent several days studying his surroundings—the stream, the bridge, and the traffic over the bridge. It was a footbridge used by people on their way to and from the village of Stenness. They were likely to carry goods and valuables.

Sadly, Gareth's moral compass had broken along with his heart. An evil plan eventually occurred to him and then consumed him. He began to hide beneath the bridge in the mornings, frightening people and robbing them of their belongings. He would grab their coattails with his powerful, twisted hands and take whatever they were carrying. If a stray animal happened upon the bridge, Gareth would snatch it up, stuff it in a sack, and take it home for dinner. Sometimes he just roared at people and animals for the hateful fun of it. "Get off my bridge or I will gobble you right up!" Then he would let out a blood-chilling cackle.

The baby was a real challenge to take care of in a cave. To feed him milk, Gareth fashioned a bag out of animal skins, and he crushed roots and berries for food until Tyson finally grew some teeth and was able to chew. When he began to crawl, his father blocked the cave entrance with rocks during waking hours so he could not get out, but otherwise he moved freely about the living space on his hands and knees. He learned to walk on the uneven earth and stone of the cave floor.

Whatever words Gareth said aloud Tyson put straight into his vocabulary bank and began to speak in his troll child voice.

As Tyson grew out of babyhood, he began to look more like his troll tribe, with a stocky body and outsized features. The red fuzz of baby hair grew thick and radiated from his head like a halo of fire.

He longed for a relationship with his father but was consistently puzzled by him. He wanted to love him; he had no one else in his young life. Why was Gareth so unreachable? What could Tyson have done to him? The boy was frequently troubled with confusion and self-doubt.

The first love a child feels is usually for his mother. Tyson had no chance to form that connection. He knew from rare conversations with Gareth that he had a very special mother named Eva. He tried to ask Gareth about her directly. "Father, could you tell me about my mother? Did she love me? What was she like? What happened to her?" He longed to know more about her, to hear stories and form a picture of her in his mind. Every now and then, Gareth would share some of his memories. "She had the most beautiful smile." If he recognized that same smile on his son's face, he never said so. And another time, "She died. She died much too soon, boy." But generally, he was just not able to open up that painful wound, and he was gruff and distant when asked about her. Over time, the two of them fell into their daily routines. Tyson prepared meals in the fireplace and kept the cave tidy while Gareth pursued his thievery and wicked behavior at the bridge.

His cruelty did not extend to Tyson. At times he even felt stirrings of affection toward his son. Sitting close to the fire at night to ward off the dank chill of the cave and speaking of nothing deeper than the weather or their evening meal, he sometimes felt the urge to put his hand on the boy's shoulder or touch his cheek. But then the reality of what Tyson had cost him would overwhelm him and he would draw back inside himself. Tyson sensed these times somehow and hope stirred in his chest, only to be snuffed out like a candle just before it has a chance to shine.

Tyson spent his spare time outside the cave studying the world above ground. The changing of the seasons delighted him. On snowy days, the bare fields gleamed white and he saw his footprints mixed with those of foxes and rabbits before the winds whipped the surface into a blank canvas once again. Most mornings, heavy sea fog wrapped the island in a ghostly, damp embrace until the near-constant wind lifted it and carried it over the high cliffs back out to the ocean.

His favorite time of year was when new growth began to pierce the cold earth of winter, announcing crops to come as spring advanced. He turned his broad face up to the same sun that helped the plants grow and imagined he could feel his mother's touch.

Spare summer hours often found him stretched out on a low stone wall, snoozing in the warmth. Skylarks and lapwings perched on his shoulder and sang their summer songs. Wildflowers bent and swayed with the rhythm of the wind. Butterflies floated past like colorful kisses.

In spite of Tyson's size and appearance, small creatures were not afraid of him. He especially loved the little brown rabbits of Orkney. They huddled at his feet while he stroked their silky ears. Sometimes he picked them up and held them close to his big body. Their tiny hearts beat within inches of his own and he savored the satisfying connection with another living creature.

The stone cottages that dotted the landscape stirred his interest. *How wonderful it must be to live in a home above the ground, to see fields and cliffs, sea and sky, sun and moon! Would that ever be possible for him?* He wondered.

People passed by but he didn't approach them. He wouldn't know what to say. He was clearly recognizable as Gareth's son and would be judged by his father's behavior. Some folks, he knew, were frightened of trolls, but he was at a loss when they pointed to his hair in horror. Gareth explained that besides being a troll his red hair was another strike against him. Many people thought redheads, or "gingers" as they were called, were witches or warlocks. Tyson knew that if he had any choice he would not spend his life in loneliness, but since he saw no alternative he depended on his cheerful nature to survive his circumstances.

One morning, as was often the case, Gareth didn't really need to steal anything. He just felt like being mean. So he nestled under the bridge in his usual spot. He shifted his weight impatiently, waiting for his first victims of the day. Eventually, three billy goats, each larger than the other, approached the bridge.

As the first one started across, Gareth roared out, "Get off my bridge or I will gobble you right up!"

"Oh, no," answered the first billy goat.

"You don't want to gobble me up. You want to wait for my brother. He is bigger than I am, and will make a better meal!"

Gareth thought for a moment and replied, "Oh, well then, go on across and be quick about it." The first billy goat crossed the bridge and waited. The second billy goat approached the troll.

"Get off my bridge or I will gobble you right up!" roared Gareth.

"Oh, no," answered the second billy goat, "You don't want to gobble me up. You want to wait for my brother. He is bigger than I am, and will make a better meal!"

Gareth once again conceded. "Oh, well then, go on across and be quick about it."

And so the third and largest billy goat started across the bridge. Once again Gareth roared, louder than ever, "Get off my bridge or I will gobble you right up!"

"Well, you just try," said the third billy goat. With that, all three goats went after Gareth and knocked him into the brook. He washed rapidly downstream and over the edge of a large waterfall. The goats waited for him to re-appear, but he never did. So they completed their crossing to the grassy meadows on the other side. A crowd of villagers standing nearby cheered so loudly that the sound brought Tyson out of the cave, curious about the commotion. Everyone got quiet.

One of the men stepped forward and gruffly announced to Tyson, "Sorry to tell you this, but those billy goats over there in the meadow just pushed your Da, your father, down the stream. He's gone over the waterfall and drowned." Shocked and speechless, Tyson just stood there, his arms dangling awkwardly at his sides. He looked first at the offending waterfall and then back at the villagers. They didn't really look sorry, and he certainly understood why. Since he had never spoken with any of them before, he wondered what he should say that would be appropriate. Finally he simply replied, "Thank you for telling me. I wouldn't have had any idea where he went and I would have waited and waited, I suppose." He raised his hand in a helpless gesture. The villagers nodded, turned and walked quietly away from the forlorn figure, feeling oddly out of the mood to celebrate.

Tyson retreated to the cave where he had spent his life with his father. It was strangely silent and lonely. He looked over at Gareth's bed, rumpled as if he had just risen from it, and was seized with deep sadness. The two of them had gotten up that morning with no idea that only one of them would be there by nightfall. Tyson wished he had said something especially kind or done something thoughtful for his father that morning, but it had just seemed like any other morning. He lay wearily down on Gareth's empty bed. His body sank into the depression left there by his father's weight until he felt enveloped and cocooned, soothed by his father's imagined embrace. But then Tyson sat up and shook his head, dismissing his fantasy. Gareth had drowned, and any chance for an affectionate relationship drowned along with him. The bereft young troll began to cry, soaking the rough pillow with tears of loss, regret, and loneliness, until he fell into an exhausted sleep.

His father's encounter with the goats left fifteen-year-old Tyson all alone. The year was 1855.

Chapter Two

Starting A New Life

In spite of his unhappy childhood spent in the shadow of his tormented father, Tyson was surprisingly different from Gareth. He was as cheerful as Gareth was bad-tempered; the sunny warmth of his heart reflected in his smile. His black eyes sparkled with intelligence, and his hair framed his face with thick crimson flames.

After the shock of Gareth's drowning had sunk in, Tyson tried to think about what to do next. With his father gone, he had no reason to stay in the cave. He was apprehensive about leaving it because it was the only home he had ever known, but there was nothing there for him now. He finally decided to start walking to Kirkwall, the village that he knew lay further down the road. He had no idea what to expect there, but he needed to move on. So, the next morning, he wrapped his few belongings in an old rag, tied them to a stick and hoisted them over his shoulder. Then, he set out from his only home with no plans ever to return.

The walk from Stenness was long and hard. When he got to Kirkwall he was hungry and thirsty, and his feet hurt. He was surprised at the beautiful stone buildings, the bustle and sound of people in the streets, and especially at all the produce and meats on display. The delicious smells reminded him of his hunger. He followed his nose to one particular establishment and asked to speak to the owner about the possibility of earning a meal. Soon a portly, middle-aged man appeared, wiping his hands on an apron that had apparently seen a very busy day. His head was frosted with curly white hair, and his broad smile put Tyson at ease.

"Good day, young fellow. I am Mr. Higbee. I own the Snooty Goose Pub. What can I do for you?"

"Sir, my name is Tyson. I have walked a very long way to get to Kirkwall. I'm hungry and thirsty, and I know the food here is delicious because I can smell it. Is there a chance you have something I could do to earn a meal?"

Mr. Higbee studied the youngster standing before him. He surely didn't know anything about him since he wasn't from Kirkwall, but he was desperately in need of a waiter. The last one had quit a month before, and he and his wife weren't really able to handle all the cooking, cleaning, washing, and waiting tables by themselves much longer. "What sort of work can you do?" he asked Tyson.

"Well, I can clean these tables and wash the dishes," he replied, sweeping his arm in the direction of the cluttered dining room. "I can mop the floors. I can even cook. I can do whatever you need me to do in exchange for dinner."

All the time Tyson was speaking, Mr. Higbee was assessing him. *Young and strong,* he thought to himself, *but a troll? A red-headed troll? Lots of folks are put off by trolls and superstitious about red hair. Call 'em gingers. Think they have supernatural powers. Hmmm.*

Just then, Tyson smiled. It transformed his wide, homely face and lit up his features in a most wonderful way. Mr. Higbee was a broad-minded man who believed in giving everyone a chance, and he made a snap decision.

"If you," said he, "are willing to serve my customers their food and drink, clean the dishes and the tables, and sometimes do the cooking when I need you, I can offer you a full-time job. I will provide you with meals, a small salary, a bed, and daily bath water." Well, Tyson didn't understand all of that, especially the bath water part, but he had taken care of his father all these years and he certainly knew how to clean and cook. He cheerfully agreed to Mr. Higbee's offer.

"Then come with me." Mr. Higbee took him back to the kitchen, sat him at the wide wooden counter and served him a big plate of *stovies*, a hearty stew of beef, potatoes, and onions. When he had enough to eat, Mr. Higbee showed him to a room upstairs in the pub, gave him a fresh towel, a washbowl of warm water, a piece of soap and instructions to sleep well and report for work in the morning. He gave Tyson a pat on the back and smiled his warm smile, then disappeared down the stairs. Tyson spent his first night freshly bathed, his belly comfortably full, on a clean straw bed in a stone building. It had been quite an amazing day. He couldn't believe his luck, finding a job like that. He fell into the deepest sleep he could ever remember.

The next morning, he awoke bright and early. For a minute he couldn't recognize where he was, but soon he remembered the events of two days ago. His thoughts turned once again to his father. He mourned his loss and the sad end of their fragile relationship. After a few moments he pulled himself back to the present, remembering he had a job to do. He patted his little bed, washed his face and dressed in the only clean clothes he owned. He went off to find Mr. Higbee. Wonderful smells were drifting up the stairs from the kitchen, and Tyson's stomach gave a tiny rumble. "Mr. Higbee," he called out. "He's out in the back, young fellow," a voice as melodious as a bird's floated on the air. "Come in and have your breakfast." A plump, smiling lady rounded the corner, her flowered apron flying, wisps of hair starting to pull away from her bun and curl into damp tendrils. "I'm Mrs. Higbee. I've heard all about you from my husband. We're glad to have you here. Let's get you fed so you can go to work. There's a lot to do today."

Tyson smiled to himself. "I've never heard a lady's voice before. It sounds just like a nightingale's song! Who ever would have imagined that?"

Mrs. Higbee directed him to a small table piled high with servings of boiled eggs, butter, cream, cheese, ham and bread. After a nod of encouragement from her, Tyson fell upon the food, wiping his plate clean with the last piece of bread. His lean years in the cave had taught him to never waste a bite.

After his meal, Mrs. Higbee directed Tyson to the sink, where he was immediately put to work. There were lots of pots, pans, and dishes to be washed, left over from the evening meal the night before. "After this, please wash the dishes at night so we'll be ready to start serving the next morning bright and early." Tyson smiled and nodded with enthusiasm. Mrs. Higbee took note of his willingness to work.

By then Mr. Higbee had appeared, dressed sensibly in workpants, leather boots and a plaid wool jacket. He pecked his wife on her rosy cheek and pumped Tyson's hand. "Good morning, young fellow. I hope you slept well. You are going to be very useful around here. Let's get started."

He took Tyson around the pub, teaching him how to set the table and where the dishes, silverware, glasses and napkins were stored. He directed him to the cleaning supplies. "We'll start here. The dining room must be spotless. Each table should be cleaned first and then set properly, like I showed you. When the customers finish their meals and leave the table, clear the dirty dishes and take them to the kitchen. The soiled linens go to the laundry room, where they are soaked and scrubbed in hot soapy water, rinsed and hung out to dry on the clotheslines behind the pub. At night when we close, wash the dishes and mop the dining room and kitchen floors so that they are ready for the next day's business."

Mr. Higbee continued, "I can see that I must advance you a little money for clothes. You can't work every day in that outfit. We'll need some shirts and trousers, and a good, sturdy pair of work shoes. We have plenty of aprons. Let's go over to McDuff's general store right now and find you something to wear." They asked Mrs. Higbee if she needed anything from the store, but she could think of nothing at the moment, so off they went down the street, enjoying the brisk air, pausing at corners to let traffic go by.

Tyson felt good inside, walking along with his new boss. He realized as Mr. Higbee made general comments about the weather and local events that he had never had an actual conversation before except for the spare ones with Gareth. Mr. Higbee asked him casual questions and he answered them, but he wasn't sure it was to ask questions of his own in return. He decided to give it a try.

"Were you born in Kirkwall, Mr. Higbee?" he ventured.

"Oh no, son, I was born in Evie, a village north of here. I came to Kirkwall to make a living, and I met the lovely lass who's now my wife. We bought the pub and here we are."

"I don't know exactly where I was born, but I grew up in a cave near Stenness," offered Tyson.

"Oh really? That sounds like an interesting story," opined Mr. Higbee. So Tyson told him all about it as they strolled down the busy street, and soon having a conversation did not seem so hard any more.

McDuff's was something he could never have imagined. It was very large and somewhat dark because there were few windows. Shelves full of items very foreign to him took up almost all the wall space. In one section there were large barrels of sugar, tins of spices, and containers of fragrant teas and coffees.

Among the bolts of fabric and suspenders they found some ready-made clothes. Tyson soon was the proud owner of two new pairs of trousers, two excellent shirts and a comfortable pair of boots.

Here, try this, Tyson," prompted Mr. Higbee, handing him a small red object covered in sugar. "What do I do with it?" "Chew it up and swallow it," chuckled his new boss. Tyson did as he was told. He was surprised when the little thing stuck to his teeth, but then the sweetness filled his mouth and he beamed. This was the moment he learned to love gumdrops, the first candy he had ever tasted.

Chapter Three

Moving On

At first Tyson was so busy at the Snooty Goose that he had little time to explore the town. But eventually he ventured out along the streets, marveling at the stores displaying art, clothing, and books. He was interested in the books from the moment he saw them. Even though the markings on the pages made no sense to him, something told him that the ability to read was very important. He had seen boys and girls passing by the pub with books in their hands, on their way to and from school, so that was the place to learn to read! How could he go there?

Fortunately for Tyson, he had proved to be a dependable, hardworking employee during the months he had been at The Snooty Goose. Both Mr. and Mrs. Higbee were very fond of him. When he asked if there was a way he could go to school, Mr. Higbee suggested that he take the mornings to go to classes. Working in the late afternoons and evenings would be enough to keep their arrangement in place.

The timing of Tyson's request was just right. A new school term was beginning the very next week. Mr. Higbee even took him to the school and made sure he was properly enrolled.

The night before his first day at school, Tyson could hardly sleep at all. He was up at five, although he didn't have to be at school until eight. He changed shirts several times, going from one to another and back again. He wondered what would happen at the school. How many others would be there? What would the teacher be like? How would they begin? How long would it take to learn to read? Mrs. Higbee called him downstairs at seven. He had been dressed and ready for two hours. "Tyson, you must eat a hearty breakfast. You have a busy day ahead and you want to be ready for it." She had prepared a delicious feast of eggs, kippers, cheese, and bread for him. As he cleaned his plate, she smiled at him with genuine pleasure and pride.

The Higbees had no bairns. It wasn't that they didn't want children. The only blight on their otherwise happy marriage was their inability to have any. It was a sad thing because their hearts would have been full of love and joy, with plans and encouragement for a child of their own.

It just wasn't meant to be.

Now Mrs. Higbee, looking at Tyson in this moment, felt for the first time the excitement and nervousness mothers feel as their children go off to their first day of school. She stood on tiptoes to give him an extra-tight hug as he went out the door and was rewarded with one of Tyson's most joyous smiles ever. She absentmindedly put her finger to her cheek as she watched him go, worrying a little about what lay in store for him. How would the other students accept him? He didn't look like them. They could make fun of his size, his red hair—and he really did not have any friends to take up for him. Perhaps she should have talked to him. "Oh, my," she fretted as he sailed off down the street toward the little stone school.

The front door of the building opened into one large room. Light from the tall windows fell upon rows of wooden desks and illuminated the rosy faces of other children. As he entered the room, Tyson saw his teacher in front of him, this wizard in granny glasses who would unlock all the wonderful, magical secrets of books for him. Tyson's dark eyes lit up, his mouth curved into as big a smile as his face could handle, and his red hair almost sizzled with excitement. Miss McNamara, in practical low-heeled shoes and a lavender dress that complimented the kind blue eyes peering from behind her little gold spectacles, smiled back at him. She knew from experience how to judge the needs and abilities of each student. Tyson, she could tell at first glance, was going to be a good one.

Miss McNamara spent much of that first day making desk assignments and acquainting the students with their supplies. They each got a reading primer, a box of chalk, and a small chalkboard with clear instructions that they were to treat these items with care. They were also encouraged to take them home to practice.

Miss McNamara had a big desk and a very large chalkboard that hung on the wall at the front of the schoolroom. Tyson held his supplies carefully in his big hands. He could hardly believe he was sitting at a school desk. He looked around at the other students and wondered if they were as excited as he was. He knew none of them, but they all seemed to know each other quite well, having grown up together in Kirkwall.

By nature friendly and open, Tyson wanted to make friends. He had noticed a few odd looks already directed at him by some of the students and rightly supposed it was because of his looks. He had long ago realized he was physically quite different from humans. He was larger, with a broad, rough face. His hair was unmanageable and he knew its color unsettled lots of people.

Suddenly feeling all quivery in his stomach, he put his head down on the desk, his thoughts clanging against the inside of his skull. Would no one like him? Was he doomed to be alone?, to be the object of fear and ridicule? Now completely unsure of himself, he raised his head and tried to focus. Miss McNamara caught his eye and winked. That calmed him down. Tyson decided that he would stick it out in the classroom, at least through the day.

The Kirkwall school was very fortunate to have Miss McNamara. She had trained for teaching in Glasgow, graduated at the top of her class, and was offered jobs in several cities; however, she wanted to return to

Orkney, where she was born. She enjoyed a warm and long-standing friendship with Mr. Slater, her teacher in Kirkwall for all the years until she went off to teacher training college. They mutually admired and respected each other, and he encouraged her to choose teaching as a profession. He had let her know when he was ready to retire, so with his blessing, she had asked for and received the job in Kirkwall.

She moved into her old room in her parents' cottage and began her life's work. Two generations of Kirkwallians were beneficiaries of her dedication. Teaching was truly her gift. She loved the opportunity and the challenge of molding children's minds and giving them the necessary tools to thrive. Teaching in a one-room school had its own unique challenges. Students were at different learning levels according to their ages, but somehow she managed to provide the personal instruction each child needed. When she was working with one of the youngsters, she focused her complete attention on that child, and her voice was kind and encouraging. She was loved by students and their parents alike.

This day, the first day of a new term, Miss McNamara smiled at her new charges, turned to the blackboard and wrote the letter **A**. Tyson's education was officially underway.

He went back the next day and the next, and then every day after that, soaking up Miss McNamara's every word. In spite of his worries about the other students, he smiled his big smile and continued to show interest in them. But just as Mrs. Higbee feared, all the children did not accept him. He was bigger and by their standards not attractive. And oh my, that red hair! Some of the children were very uncomfortable and even frightened of him because of it. However, he continued to be open and friendly with the other students, and eventually many of them—won over by his irrepressible good humor— warmed up to him.

His special friend was a boy named Corky, who sat in front of him in the schoolroom. He was a small-boned boy whose brown hair nestled close to his scalp like bird feathers. Freckles danced across his turned-up nose. Corky was a quiet boy, but Tyson, who had by now mastered the art of conversation, kept asking him questions. "Were you born in Kirkwall?" "Do you have brothers and sisters?" "Can you already read, or are you just learning?" Corky began to answer him and respond with his own questions, and soon they knew all about each other. Before long they became good friends. They began to walk to and from school together every day.

One afternoon several months into the school session, he and Corky were on their way home, skipping and hopping in the puddles left from an earlier rain and laughing as friends do. Suddenly, Tyson became aware of a shadow at his elbow. He turned to see one of his classmates standing there. It was Ozzie Grogan, a dirty, unkempt, unpleasant boy who always seemed angry at the world. Ozzie pushed him hard and Tyson, off-balance, fell to the wet ground. "Hey, Ozzie," Corky cried out, "What did you do that for?" Ozzie glared at them; his brown eyes snapped with anger. "That big ginger ape," he yelled, "That ugly carrot top! He thinks he's so smart! I'm going to teach him a thing or two."

With that, he grabbed Tyson's chalkboard from his hand and broke it against a fence. "That's just for starts, troll. You'd better go back to that cave you came from, or I'll make you wish you had!" Then, he turned and disappeared down the street.

Tyson was horrified by Ozzie's yelling and pushing, but more by the broken slate. How could he tell Miss McNamara that he had not protected school property? How could he tell the Higbees? Tears welled in his eyes, to his shock and surprise. He hadn't cried since the day Gareth died, and he didn't want to do it now. But he couldn't help it.

His friend gave him a hand up. Both were visibly shaken. They continued on in silence to the pub where Corky turned left toward his own home and Tyson, ashen-faced, ducked his head and hurried upstairs to the safety of his room. This was a nightmare. Why couldn't Ozzie accept him or at least just leave him alone? What was he to do about his broken chalkboard? He put the pieces on his bed, washed his face, changed his soiled clothes and went downstairs to work, planning to say nothing about today's incident until he had time to think.

The next day, Corky stopped for him as usual, and Tyson hoped that what had happened the day before was just a one-time occurrence. He didn't want to lie to Miss McNamara about the chalkboard, but neither did he want to tell the whole truth. When she noticed the broken board and asked him about it he replied, "I'm so sorry, ma'am. I fell down and it got broken."

With that Ozzie, who was lurking nearby, gave a hateful snigger. Miss McNamara silently took notice of it.

"Well, it will have to be replaced," announced Tyson's teacher. "I'll send to Stromness for another one. I know it was an accident and that you will take special care of the new one." Tyson breathed a sigh of relief and turned his attention to his schoolwork.

On the way home in the afternoon, Ozzie appeared again, accompanied by two more boys chanting, "Ginger! Ginger! Big fat ginger!" Tyson and Corky walked quickly past them and ignored the taunts and jeers as best they could. They reached the pub and both went inside. Mrs. Higbee, waiting inside the door, heard the commotion and demanded to know what was happening. "Oh, that boy Ozzie is mad at me; I don't know why. Today we just hurried home and didn't pay any attention to him and the others." Mrs. Higbee studied them, thinking about that. Then she said, "You say you did that today. Has something happened before today?" Oh, you could never fool Mrs. Higbee.

Corky piped up, "Yesterday, Ozzie pushed him down and broke his chalkboard. He was alone then, but now there are other boys with him."

"Well I never!" cried Mrs. Higbee. "Tyson, you need to let Miss McNamara know about this. You handled it the right way this afternoon. Walk away from them; don't try to talk to them. They want to know they've got your attention. Without it they may get tired of the bullying. Remember, Tyson, Ozzie has some difficulties. There are a lot of children in that family. The father's job as a fosser doesn't provide much money. And something about his job—being the town gravedigger—makes folks nervous around the Grogans."

Mrs. Higbee continued, "You boys are both better off walking together rather than alone. Tyson, if you need to talk more about this you can come to me any time."

School went on, and so did the bullying. Not every day, but often enough. Tyson got his new chalkboard. Though he hid it under his jacket, those troublemakers grabbed him and got hold of it, and Ozzie smashed it against the fence. This time, Tyson had to tell Miss McNamara what had happened. She didn't seem surprised, and a strange shadow passed across her face.

She kept Ozzie after school several times and talked to him about his behavior, trying to help him put a name to his own insecurities that compelled him to bully Tyson. She knew, of course, that unlike Tyson, he struggled academically and seldom did his homework. She suspected that his home life was chaotic and undisciplined. She knew how most people in town viewed his family and understood how that might give rise to a rage in him. But he firmly resisted her efforts to help him, and the bullying continued.

Miss McNamara began to see the effects of it on Tyson. He was quiet, and with the exception of Corky, he stopped seeking out his friends. His eyes lost their lively expression and his shoulders drooped with self-doubt. She could not bear it. One Friday she took him aside. "Sadly, Tyson," she told him, "there are people who can only be happy when they spoil other people's joy. And sometimes special measures have to be taken…"

That weekend Tyson was busy at the pub and thoughts of Ozzie faded. On Monday as he and Corky started to school, he saw Ozzie rushing toward him, his arm raised as if to strike. Suddenly he dropped to his haunches and looked up imploringly at the two boys from his position at their feet. "Ribbit," he croaked. "Ribbit."

Tyson and Corky were stumped. What in the world was this about? But they kept their mouths shut and walked on. Soon they heard Ozzie running behind them. He dashed in front and turned, raising his fist. Down he dropped again, squatting and croaking, "Ribbit. Ribbit."

This went on for two weeks. Every time he approached them aggressively, Ozzie suddenly behaved exactly like a frog, and he was helpless to stop it. His previous companions quickly abandoned him, and soon the whole town was buzzing about his behavior.

"Never seen anything like this before," mused one man. But an old-timer recalled a bully from Mr. Slater's class about thirty years back who barked like a dog for several weeks and then became a model citizen— thoughtful and kind, hardworking and generous, with a special soft spot for any victim of bullying. At that, several more remembered having been in school with that boy and marveled at the amazing change that had taken place in him. They remembered they had come to like and even admire him.

Miss McNamara smiled. She remembered the day she returned to Orkney and met with her friend and mentor Mr. Slater. After they had discussed the general information about her new job, he pressed a small wooden box into her hand. "My dear, I hope you will never need this box. My own teacher gave it to me when I began my career. I only used the contents once in all these years, when the situation seemed unsolvable any other way." He continued, looking her steadily in the eye, "We are teachers, not sorcerers. But sometimes with certain students special measures must be taken. This box contains a unique tool for stopping cruel behavior and helping the offender reach a clearer way of thinking. It is not meant to inflict irreparable damage to the wrongdoer in the way his bullying can do to his victims. It is a last resort teaching tool. A dose of humility. If the bully has any conscience at all, it will work, and he'll be better for it in the long run." Miss McNamara looked down at the little box. A tin label screwed to the cover read, "Spells For Use On Recalcitrant Bullies."

After several weeks of enduring the Frog Spell, Ozzie finally came to understand the pain he had inflicted on Tyson, because he was experiencing it himself. It was the pain of being taunted for something he could not change. Tyson could change neither his red hair nor his trollness, and now Ozzie couldn't change his ludicrous froggy behavior even though people were laughing at him, he went to Miss McNamara with his head bowed. "I see now that what I was doing was mean and I'm sorry for it. I haven't ever asked anybody for any kind of help but I've got to do it now. Miss McNamara, can you help me apologize to Tyson? I've never said I was sorry to anybody, so it's going to be hard. And can you help me with my schoolwork too? I don't want to be a dumb kid. I just don't know how to do it better."

Miss McNamara took Ozzie's face between her hands and looked into his distressed face. "You will have to make your apology to Tyson yourself. Only you can do that. But my hunch is that he will accept it gladly. I'm happy you are interested in improving your schoolwork. Now, I always found it helpful to study with another person after school. Sometimes I understood something my study partner didn't, and sometimes it was the other way around, so it helped us both. Why don't we see if Tyson could find some time to study with you? I think his work schedule is fairly heavy, but the Higbees are flexible about anything to do with school. Maybe you two can help each other."

Ozzie left the school and went straight to find Tyson before he lost his nerve. Tyson was alarmed at the sight of him, but when Ozzie remained on his feet and spoke civilly, he knew something had changed. Of course, Miss McNamara was right. Tyson happily accepted the apology and agreed to find time to study with Ozzie. He was all for anybody who was trying to learn. Over the rest of the term and for many terms after that, they studied together in the afternoons. Ozzie made steady progress in their school subjects under the influence of Tyson's enthusiasm and dedication, and regular study time at the pub, outside the noise and chaos of his own home, gave him a chance to learn the value of self-discipline. The two became fast friends, and Ozzie made it his mission from that time forward to defend anybody who was bullied.

Chapter Four

The Fairy

Tyson worked hard for the next six years at the Snooty Goose, and all the while his life changed dramatically—six short years to recover the fifteen lost to loneliness and ignorance. At the pub he learned the principles for running a successful business. All during that time he continued to attend the school. He had long ago mastered reading and writing, as well as math, and moved on to bookkeeping, history and science. He had learned to cook as a necessity, but along the way he developed quite an interest in it and indulged himself in the pleasure of experimenting with new and unusual combinations of ingredients.

The pub patrons were always willing samplers of his concoctions, which often became a part of the Snooty Goose's expanding menu. He created a number of dishes to be served at Hogmanay, the most celebrated Scottish holiday, observed on December 31 each year. Before he had come to Kirkwall, he knew nothing of the holiday. He had seen torches placed outside the small cottages near the cave at the darkest time of year, but he had no idea why they were put there.

Mr. Higbeee explained that the Hogmanay celebration heralded coming relief from the winter darkness. A student of astronomy, he related the concept of the earth turning on its axis around the sun. When countries located in the northern half, or hemisphere, of the earth were tilted away from the sun, colder temperatures and darker days occurred. At the Winter Solstice, the shortest day of the year, daylight in Scotland lasted only about seven hours. After that, the hours of daylight increased as the earth's axis began to tilt that hemisphere back toward the sun. Daylight began to last longer and temperatures began to grow warmer.

Each year on the last day of December, Scottish citizens, weary of the cold and dark, built fires to symbolize the coming of light and the spring season. They put torches out and opened their homes to welcome friends, family and neighbors. Ample food was prepared for all visitors and gifts were exchanged.

Tyson had enjoyed the celebration with the Higbees ever since he had come to live with them. He and Mrs. Higbee started their own special tradition of baking a gingerbread house to set out in the front hall of the pub. For them it was a symbol of their hospitality, a welcome into their home. Tyson loved Hogmanay, and the house he and Mrs. Higbee fashioned from cookies and candy had special significance to him as a symbol of a place where he had found acceptance.

When the pub was closed on Sunday afternoons, he was a regular at concerts and lectures sponsored by the Arts Council. Music, especially piano and violin, touched him deeply. He had an intense appreciation for painting. Personalities, subjects, methods and materials fascinated him and he never missed a lecture.

Eventually, his interest led him to start taking oil painting lessons. He stretched his own canvases on blocks of wood and ordered his paints from Edinburgh. His familiarity with the structure of animals and plants of Orkney gave him a good understanding of his favorite subject matter, and he became a very proficient painter.

He studied a great deal about the Old Masters, as they were called, the acclaimed European painters who produced the bulk of their work before 1800. He especially admired the Italian painters: Botticelli, Da Vinci, and Michelangelo, as well as the great Dutch artist Hieronymus Bosch, French painters Poussin and Delacroix, Spanish artist Francisco Goya, and Britain's Sir Joshua Reynolds. They produced glowing canvases rendered so realistically that the figures seemed made of flesh, ready to step out of their richly depicted backgrounds right into the room with him.

He felt a special connection with Sir Joshua Reynolds because he had taken a young, talented painter from Stenness as a pupil in London and trained him in the art of portrait painting. That young man, by the unremarkable name of Charles Smith, had gone on to be court painter for the Grand Mogul in India. Imagine that this could happen to an Orkney lad! It seized Tyson's interest and made the Old Masters relevant to him.

Mr. Higbee and his wife had begun to consider Tyson family. He was quick-witted, talented and hardworking, so they decided to give him a share in the pub. They reasoned that this arrangement would be good for both them and Tyson. They were growing older and were not as spry as they had been in their younger years. Tyson was by now highly regarded by people in town, who had affectionately begun to call him Ty. He had a natural talent for cooking and bookkeeping as well as an easy manner with customers. And, the Higbees loved him. That fact had become quite happily clear to them.

One could hardly recognize him as the young, shabby fellow who had come to town some six years earlier. He was clean and well-dressed, well-spoken and well-mannered. He had a keen appreciation for art, music, and history. He had a large, lively circle of friends, including the once hostile Ozzie as well as his faithful friend Corky.

An old idea resurfaced in Ty's mind—the idea of a home of his own. He remembered the early days when he observed the occasional small cottages near the bridge. They looked cheerful and warm, with light glowing inside and smoke curling from the chimneys. Through the windows there had to have been beautiful views—crops and flowers, sunlight and mist, moon and stars. He had wondered if he would ever have a chance to live that way.

Now he knew that it was possible. Ty tucked the idea back inside his busy head, where only the fiery hair that crowned it remained the same.

One day, Ty was on his way to the library to check out a book about the artist Rembrandt when he noticed a shiny silver carriage waiting near the entrance. He was certain he hadn't seen it before. It was not a sight someone would forget. Who in Kirkwall would have such a fine coach? A cart or wagon, perhaps, or even a wooden carriage, but not one designed in precious metal.

Ty set the thought aside and returned to his mission, browsing on his way to the Arts Section. He rounded a corner and found himself paralyzed, rooted to the spot. Before him was the most exquisite creature he could ever imagine. She was creamy and blushing, and her wings trembled slightly as her eyes met his. Her eyes were the color of the summer sky, blue and clear. He was struck by the kindness in her face. Who was she?

Ty had never seen wings on anything but birds and bugs. Hers were delicately veined, with rainbow colors that changed in the light. Her hair, dusted with gold and moonbeams, drifted gently around her slender shoulders. She smiled and then dropped her gaze shyly. Ty stood like stone, his big grin pasted to his face. He was helpless as she moved past him and through the library door. He saw her step into the exquisite silver carriage he had seen earlier. Light gleamed and bounced from its elegant surfaces as it pulled away from the curb. Never had he seen any kind of transportation so beautifully crafted.

When it was out of sight, he began to think he was dreaming. Could the girl have possibly been real, standing between the rows of bookcases like any everyday human? Then it struck him. She was not human. What was she? How and where could he ever see her again?

He returned to the pub in a daze, not even remembering how he got there. As soon as he saw Mr. Higbee, he was full of questions. "Mr. Higbee, I have just seen the most beautiful girl in the whole world. Have you ever seen a girl with wings? This one had wings, Mr. Higbee. She was at the library. She left in a silver carriage. *A silver carriage.*"

Mr. Higbee smiled kindly at the agitated lad. He truly loved Ty, and he was pleased to see him interested in something other than work and art. "Well, Ty, the best thing for you to do is go right back to the library and ask for a book about fairies. They are a different tribe from humans like me and trolls like you. They take some studying. I have heard that a wealthy fairy family has built a new home not far from town. They could certainly afford transportation by silver carriage. This beautiful creature must belong to them."

Ty's eyes grew wide and he shook his head. "Oh no, Mr. Higbee, that's not possible," he exclaimed, "I have heard terrible things about fairies!" He was recalling old wives' tales passed from generation to generation in Orkney regarding trolls and fairies that were repeated to him by his father. "True, I have never seen one, but I know they are sometimes feared as much as trolls! She cannot be a fairy! I plainly saw the goodness in her face!"

"Ty, you know as well as I do that there are bad trolls as well as bad humans and probably bad fairies too. But you are a good troll, and you have changed many minds in Kirkwall about trolls in general because of your kindness and intelligence. Our customers consider you a friend. They enjoy your good mind and your pleasant manner with them. Miss McNamara considers you her prize pupil. Mrs. Higbee and I appreciate your loyalty and your generous heart. Mr. McDuff likes you and he trusts you enough to let you have your own account in his store. If you saw goodness in this fairy I believe you can trust your instincts. Go get your book and I'll keep my ears open in case I hear anything more about these fairy folk."

Ty ran back to the library as fast as his feet would carry him. The librarian directed him to the section on Ancient Civilizations, and after some rummaging, he found exactly what he wanted: an illustrated history of fairies. There they were, shining from the pages, some with wings like dragonflies, some with wings like butterflies. There were males and females alike, agile, fragile, and altogether beautiful. Ty was bursting with excitement and with something else—a desire to see that fairy again. Something had turned in his heart, he knew, and he was now forever changed.

The week dragged by impossibly slowly while Ty tended to his affairs and hoped for another glimpse of her. He saw the silver carriage pass by the pub several times, but he could not see inside it.

One day Mr. Higbee called him back into the office. "Ty," he said, "I asked the town registrar, Mr. Leith, about the fairy family and learned that they go by the name of Fleming. They are nobility. The father is a member of the fairy Royal Family. An Earl, I believe. Lord and Lady Fleming are parents of only one child, a girl. Her name is Amelia. She must be the one you saw. Lord Fleming was born in Orkney, and now they have retired here. Their house is off the road to Stromness. I hope this helps you."

Ty retired to his room in the evening with his mind full of Amelia. Amelia. Now he knew her name. He slept well that night and dreamed of her, the sun slipping through her golden hair, her gossamer wings casting lovely shadows across her face, and her blue eyes gazing directly into his soul.

On Sunday, Ty attended a lecture on the Italian painter, Michelangelo. He had studied illustrations of his work in his collection of art books and considered him one of the most important artists of Italy. He had just settled in his chair when Amelia drifted into the room, lifted slightly from the floor by her delicate rainbow wings. She was followed by another fairy, more plainly dressed, who he supposed must be her maidservant. They took seats near the lecturer, and Ty had a clear view of her delicate profile. She was as lovely as he remembered.

"She must be interested in the arts, just as I am," he thought. "Maybe that will be our common ground!" Cheered by the thought, he waited impatiently for the end of the lecture so he could get to her before she left.

When she saw him, she smiled in recognition; she remembered him from the library. Ty introduced himself and asked if she had enjoyed the lecture. They fell into easy conversation. She was quite knowledgeable about painting, and turned out to be a music lover as well.

"I look forward to the Sunday performances that are coming up," she told him. "My family encourages my interest, and I am allowed to attend these events on my own, accompanied only by my personal maid." Ty glowed at the realization that he would have other opportunities to be with her and that they had common ground indeed. Every Sunday for the next few months found Ty at every scheduled event, watching for the silver carriage.

When Amelia was there they continued their lively conversations, enjoying each other's company immensely and growing more deeply connected. She never once seemed uneasy at his appearance and looked him directly in the eye with only interest and pleasure showing in her face. That meant the world to him, and it helped him to be himself with her. They used the time after the arts presentations to learn more about each other, and each time Amelia's maid waited for her patiently outside, pleased that her mistress had a friend.

Amelia told Ty about her upbringing in London. The family had access to museums (where she had seen many of the actual paintings they discussed in their Sunday Arts Council lectures) and theatres, to the salons where authors, musicians, artists, and politicians gathered to discuss current events. She and her parents had even been to Buckingham Palace on occasion by invitation of Queen Victoria. Her privileged life could have made Ty doubt even more his chances with her, but her genuine warmth and attention sent him a different message, so he pushed the thought aside and continued to seek her company. She confessed that she had been lonely in Orkney until she met Ty. During their conversations, he learned that she had been an excellent student with a particular interest in history and the arts. She had planned to teach in London, but then the family retired to Orkney.

"Perhaps you can teach in Kirkwall, Amelia," said Ty. "Miss McNamara, who was my teacher, will be retiring before long."

Amelia's face lit up with pleasure. "I would like to contribute something to the world, Ty. I want to serve a purpose. I believe that the best way I can do that is through teaching. Can you help me find out if that would be possible in Kirkwall?"

"Of course," he smiled, "I will speak to Miss McNamara very soon." He was delighted to have a chance to help her answer her calling.

Over time, Ty told her all about his past. He recounted the loss of his mother and the difficulty of growing up in a cave with his father. He told her about Gareth's encounter with the billy goats and his drowning. He spoke lovingly of the Higbees, who had become the parents he had never had. He told her of his illiteracy and his ignorance of the importance of an education when he first arrived in Kirkwall. He described his excitement when Mr. Higbee made it possible for him to go to school and smiled as he spoke of Miss McNamara and the marvelous world she created in that one schoolroom.

Amelia's eyes misted as she listened to Ty. What different lives the two of them had led! She had been pampered and adored while he suffered from loneliness and ignorance. But he had the courage to face one obstacle after another to build a life for himself. She admired him greatly and had begun to care deeply for him. Ty knew when he saw her in the library that he was going to fall in love with her. What he didn't know was that at that same encounter she had looked directly past his appearance, straight into his kind and loving heart. She too was smitten.

Chapter Five

A Terrible Day

Spring arrived. It was Ostrefest at St. Magnus Cathedral in Kirkwall. Everyone came from surrounding villages to perform in the orchestral concerts and operas or simply to hear and enjoy them. Ty looked forward to the festival more than usual because he hoped to enjoy it with Amelia.

The first day he attended the festival he saw no sign of her, and the sunny day turned grey. The second day she was there. She wore a finely tucked be ribboned gown and held a delicate lace parasol above her fair face to shade it from the sun. When she caught sight of him her face lit up with pleasure. Ty gave a formal bow. "My dear Amelia, how lovely you look today! You take my breath away!"

From behind her stepped a courtly, dignified fairy, most obviously her father, Lord Magnus Fleming. "What is your name, sir?" he asked. "And how do you suppose that you can speak to my daughter in such a familiar way?" As Ty prepared to introduce himself to Lord Fleming, it suddenly occurred to him that he had no last name. What a completely unexpected realization...awkward in the extreme!

Visions of his life with his fierce and heartless father in the cave, eating berries, roots and wild animals, forced their way into his mind. He suddenly thought to himself that he had no right at all to even try to know this lovely fairy. He had no right at all to present himself, his shabby, ungainly self, to her righteously protective father. His shoulders sagged momentarily, but then Amelia reached out and rested her slender fingers on his forearm as lightly as thistle down, and he rallied.

To her father he said, "My name is Tyson. I am a troll, therefore, I have no last name. But I have finished my schooling; I have a good head for business. I intend to be so successful in life that I will have the right to choose my own last name. Sir, I ask your permission to call upon your daughter." Amelia, startled by his request, smiled a happy smile.

Lord Fleming scowled at Ty. His moustache drew down to frame a deep frown. Amelia immediately realized his obvious displeasure. Her delicate wings trembled and her smile faded.

Ty looked into the furious face of Amelia's father and even his fiery hair paled and drooped slightly. "Why, you impudent twit!" roared the Earl, "You immensely foolish fellow! I would never allow you to come anywhere near my daughter! You are not our kind. You are a troll, probably as dimwitted as the rest of them. You are entirely beneath her station! Say no more. Get out of my sight and never trouble me or my daughter again!" With that, he seized Amelia by the elbow and steered her quickly down the street, away from the disheartened Ty.

Amelia glanced behind her as they hurried toward their carriage and saw the terrible harm her father's words had caused. Ty was looking after them, his shoulders drooping, his eyes dark with pain, his joy snuffed out like a candle. Her heart ached.

Ty was so shocked that he had to rest a minute on the street. His head felt as if it were full of buzzing black flies. How could he abandon his dream of Amelia?

Well, I cannot forget her. I cannot give up. I don't know how to work this out yet, so I will do what I know best for now, thought Ty. *I will work harder than ever. I will make a success of myself. I intend to make Amelia my wife.* He was startled by the thought, but then he realized that he absolutely meant what he said.

I will somehow prove to Lord Fleming that I can provide generously for his daughter. Perhaps I will give her a wonderful home and fill it with love for her. His dream of a house had stayed in his mind. He knew he would build it for himself. Now he thought it might be for Amelia as well.

Just thinking about it dulled the pain of the afternoon and sharpened his resolve. He returned to the Snooty Goose and rolled up his sleeves. There was much to do, and much to think about.

Chapter Six

Hurting Hearts

In the days that followed, what was becoming of Amelia? How had she reacted to the dreadful encounter between her father and Ty on Broad Street? Well, it was heartbreaking. She thought of Ty every waking moment. She could see his merry, kind eyes and his contagious grin. Even though they were apart, she sensed the warmth of his fiery red hair and most especially of his generous heart. She had never felt this way before. She had attracted many suitors in London, but no one had even come close to capturing her heart. They seemed very dull compared to Ty. Somehow he was bigger than life. His skin could hardly contain his enthusiasm, his joyous spirit, his curiosity, determination, and devotion. She knew that she wanted only him.

Under her father's harsh judgment and intolerance, she began to shrink ever so slightly. The iridescence of her wings dulled and her hair lost its golden luster. She spoke little and cried often. She came to the dining room for evening meals with her parents, but she did not join in their attempts at conversation. The rest of the time, she stayed in her room and thought of Ty. At night she looked through her window at the moon and wondered if he saw it and thought of her.

Her father and mother were very worried about her. They had the doctor from Kirkwall come out to examine her for illness, but he found nothing physically wrong. "Frankly, sir," he advised, "Your daughter's health is good. My diagnosis would be that she is suffering from melancholia."

Lord Fleming had told his wife of the Ostrefest encounter, and they both realized that it had upset Amelia, but what could they do? In family matters her father always had the last word, and in his view he had spoken it.

Members of the fairy royal family were destined for marriage to others of their same aristocratic station. It had always been that way. For his daughter to marry a troll would, in Lord Fleming's estimation, destroy her future. She would be left out of their social circles. She would be forever rejected by the privileged world into which she was born. Lord Fleming found that thought too hard to bear. He loved his daughter. It was his duty to protect her. As much as it upset him to see her suffering, he was firm in his determination to keep Ty out of her life at any cost.

In time he would have to consider that cost. Burdened by her father's intractability in the face of her own wishes and by the forced separation from Ty, Amelia continued to decline. She developed an alarming fever. She seemed to have lost the strength to fight her father's prejudice and instead stayed in her bed, shivering and coughing.

The doctor visited daily but could not reverse her downward spiral. Her mother spent her days and nights at Amelia's bedside, patiently bathing her forehead with cool water and murmuring motherly words of encouragement to her only child. Amelia became delirious. When she spoke, her murmurings made little sense. From time to time she asked for Ty, but her father ignored the requests. He could not bring himself to let that troll into his home, so he told himself that she did not know what she was saying.

One day, Ty saw the silver carriage stop at the pharmacy down the street, leave again quickly and vanish around the corner. Alarmed, he hurried to the shop and asked the pharmacist why it had been there. "To get medication for the daughter." he replied, "She is quite seriously ill."

Ty's eyes grew wide. He sagged against the counter, his heart hammering on his ribs. Amelia? Ill? What was the matter? He dashed back to the pub, told Mrs. Higbee what he had learned, then ran down the Stromness Road all the way to the Fleming home, where he knocked frantically at the door. A servant swung it open.

"Please, I must see Lady Amelia. I need to know that she will recover from her illness!" Lord Fleming appeared from the depths of the grand hall. "Leave at once!" he roared.

"Oh please sir, no. Please let me see Lady Amelia. Please tell me what is wrong with her, I beg you."

"You have been told before. You are not welcome in our lives. That will not change." With that Lord Fleming shut the door firmly in Ty's face.

Ty sat down on the stone steps, miserable and unable to move any farther. For the third time in his life, tears streamed down his face. He finally rose and stumbled back to the road, where he remained for the rest of the day and night, as if his presence might in some way shield Amelia from further harm. He tried in vain to stave off thoughts of losing her the way he had lost his mother. He did not think he could bear another loss so profound.

Suddenly he understood his father's all-consuming grief, the grief that destroyed his heart and rendered him incapable of feeling. Ty loved Amelia as dearly as Gareth had loved Eva. If she did not recover would he be any stronger than his father had been? Would his grief overwhelm him and turn him to stone? Was his father happy and smiling before the world came down and crushed his soul? Ty did not know the answers to those questions. He bowed his head in despair.

There was no movement at the house and he knew Lord Fleming would never let him come in. When the sun rose, he walked back to the pub and collapsed in exhaustion. Mrs. Higbee fed him some warm breakfast and tried to comfort him, but he was inconsolable. Who did he think he was, anyway? A ginger-haired troll who grew up in a cave with a criminal father, without a mother, without friends. Without even a last name!

Her father saw him as he truly was, an obstacle to Amelia's happiness. He didn't deserve her. When he saw himself through Lord Fleming's eyes, he was horrified. He worried and he grieved, and then he vowed to honor Lord Fleming's wishes. He would make no further attempt to see Amelia.

Still, each night after he finished work, he walked or caught rides with travelers on the road and spent the night at the edge of the Fleming property, watching Amelia's window and praying for her recovery. If she could just survive, he would live with the fact that she could not be in his life. How he would do it, he didn't know, but he knew that he could not bear her death.

Late one moon-drenched night, as he lay drifting in and out of sleep in the damp grass, he thought he saw Lord Fleming's silver coach leave the carriage house. Harnessed to it was a snow white horse with huge feathered wings. He rubbed his eyes, astonished, but when he looked again he saw only their brown Clydesdale and decided he had gone to sleep momentarily and dreamed it. The carriage pulled behind the buildings on the property and disappeared from sight.

In a moment, Ty saw something else that made him question his sanity. From the back of the buildings, a shooting star rocketed into the sky, rapidly gaining distance from the gravity of earth. But wasn't it going the wrong way? Shouldn't it be falling rather than climbing? He could make no sense of it, so he returned to thoughts of the carriage. It was an odd time for a midnight trip and he started to worry about whether it had anything to do with the doctor or the druggist.

Amelia's mother had spoken plainly to Lord Fleming of her anxiety about her daughter. Now she was thinking only of Amelia's survival. There was one thing her husband could do to ease their minds, and it directly involved the carriage.

The silver coach was of great importance to the Flemings. It was beautiful, but its beauty was a very small part of its value to them. It was one of the most powerful tools on earth—one that kings and queens would give their crowns for but would never be able to own. The carriage gave the Flemings the ability to travel in time.

Lord Fleming inherited it from his father, who had inherited it from his own father. Their ancestors were members of the exclusive time travel society *Tempus Fugit*, a Latin name meaning "Time Flies." Each member had his own form of transportation. The Flemings' was, in fact, the beautiful silver coach. Its mysterious power was channeled through a large double-pointed crystal that charged it, giving it the ability to move forward or backward in time. As Time Travelers, all members took a solemn oath to guard the secrets of coveted membership in *Tempus Fugit*.

Zeus, the family Clydesdale, was no ordinary steed, but a magical horse, of course! He was in reality the fabled winged horse Pegasus in disguise. This mythological animal had lived for centuries, and Lord Fleming's family had been lucky enough to acquire him. The horse moved with the carriage through the succession of owners. On the occasion of a trip into time, Pegasus would reveal his true identity, spread his wings and lift the carriage beyond the sky into the lanes that led to the past or the future.

Lord Fleming only made use of this gift under the cover of night to lessen the chance of discovery. He had used it often for purposes of education, pleasure or just out of curiosity, but never for a purpose as fraught with fear as this one. That night, his wife had begged him to visit the future in order to learn their daughter's fate. Amelia's mother was exhausted physically and emotionally and nearing a breaking point. She was willing to risk learning the worst for a chance at relief from this agony. She would not go with him, for she could not bear to leave Amelia. The anguish in her tired eyes, convinced him. As frightened as he was for Amelia, he was now frightened for his wife as well. He agreed to go, and headed for the carriage house where he quickly harnessed the horse to the silver coach. Pegasus transported him through the vast and luminous cloud of the Milky Way to the hole in the sky and with a boom they exploded into the celestial lanes in a matter of minutes. The trip into the future was underway. They traveled swiftly through swirling colors of galaxies and the birth and death of stars. They rocketed through black holes and emerged into blinding light. Stars showered down on them as they searched for their destination.

Meanwhile, Lady Fleming looked out of Amelia's window at the lone, faithful figure at the corner of the property. Her mind was a tangle of fear and confusion. She was well aware of her husband's opposition to the troll, but she also knew that his presence might spark the beginning of Amelia's recovery. Never had she defied Lord Fleming. Her daughter was in crisis, however, and that propelled her to a bold decision.

She hurried down to the edge of their property where Ty sat and invited him to come in. Astounded but grateful, he rose and followed her into the house and upstairs to Amelia's room.

Tyson found Amelia tucked under a silky comforter but her curls spilled over her pillow to frame her exquisite face, a face pale enough now to break his heart. He approached her bed and took her delicate hand in his big gentle one.

"Oh Amelia, please come back. You are so loved. I am so worried for you." His familiar voice penetrated the lonely place where her mind had gone. Color rose in her cheeks and her eyelids fluttered. "I am waiting for you. I will wait for you forever." Amelia stirred and smiled weakly, signaling to Ty and her mother that she heard his voice.

Lady Fleming, relieved and newly alive with hope, embraced Ty and thanked him for his loyalty. "I am so grateful to you, young man. I am hopeful my daughter might begin to recover now. But I need to ask a favor of you and I hope you will understand why. For the present, could we keep your visit just between us? I need to find the right moment to tell my husband. He will not be rational about this right now."

Ty readily agreed. He did not want to cause Lady Fleming further anxiety. There had been quite enough for everyone already. Amelia's reaction to his voice had given him new hope as well, and that was sufficient for now.

Meanwhile Lord Fleming had reached his destination in the future. He searched the parade of images filtering like constantly moving shadows through that starry space and finally saw his daughter, lovely and blooming, smiling at someone. Who was it?

Oh, no! His stomach lurched at the sight of Ty, the cursed troll. He was there too. Lord Fleming knew the cardinal rule of *Tempus Fugit*. As a Time Traveler, he could only observe; he could not alter the course of events. The only changes he could make were in his own behavior or conviction as a result of what he saw, and he was in no state to think about that right now. He was relieved at the knowledge that Amelia would survive, but although he was helpless to change it, he could not accept the troll's presence in her future. He returned home in turmoil and reported to his wife only that Amelia would live. She in turn did not tell him of Ty's visit. So each now kept a burdensome secret from the other.

Amelia began to regain some strength. Her father's visits to her bedside were strained, although he assured her over and over of his love for her. If he loved her, she wondered, why couldn't he see that his pride and stubbornness were in large part the reason for her illness? She would get well. She wanted to get well. She had heard Ty's dear voice through the dark fog of her long night. She had to find a way to reconcile her father to her feelings for him.

Lady Fleming managed to have a message delivered to Ty at the Snooty Goose concerning Amelia's improvement. His prayers had been answered, and for that, he was grateful.

Chapter Seven

Lightning Strikes

During the time he had been with the Higbees and had moved from cooking for joy to developing recipes in earnest, Ty had concocted a very special recipe he considered superior to any of his others. It was a well-known favorite in Scotland, but he had tweaked and perfected his own special recipe for sticky toffee pudding. He tested it on the Higbees, his friends Corky and Ozzie, and on Miss McNamara, who was always there to support him. He had fiddled with the ingredients until he had a sticky toffee pudding of which people were beginning to take notice.

As word of its unique deliciousness spread, customers began to come from all over Orkney, even from the furthest islands. Now that Amelia was recovering from her illness and he had time to devote to a new endeavor, Ty decided it was time to start his own business. He devised a plan to supply the pudding to restaurants and pubs other than the Snooty Goose, and now, with the Higbees' blessing, he decided it was time to put his plan in motion.

Ty wanted to export the pudding to mainland Scotland and to England. He made arrangements with carton makers and shippers and establishments outside of Orkney who placed orders for the dessert. Soon he began to receive more orders, even from faraway places like Italy and the United States of America! His bank account grew large and comfy thanks to his thriftiness. Ty had wanted his own home all his life. He was determined to save enough to build the home he had in mind. When he grew weary, he visualized that house, and it renewed his strength.

Never was Amelia far from his thoughts. As she recovered, he dedicated himself to his business with renewed vigor. Thanks to Lady Fleming's recognition of him, some of his confidence returned. He saw her as a possible ally in the effort to change Lord Fleming's opinion. After his visit to Amelia, Ty knew he wasn't a burden on her heart. If that had been so she would not have smiled when she heard his voice. As soon as she was strong enough, she would surely ask about him and he fully intended to see her at the first opportunity. How or where he didn't know. He would just have to leave that to fate. Meanwhile, he worked tirelessly at the pub, waiting tables during the day and baking all night.

The demand for Ty's sticky toffee pudding increased by leaps and bounds. It was shipped from the port at

Stromness, some distance from Kirkwall. There were so many orders he had to lease a wagon and a Clydesdale horse to transport the product to the port, where it shipped from Orkney to its faraway destinations.

Ty set out from Kirkwall early one morning. The wagon was loaded with cartons of pudding and the weather looked promising after the winds lifted the early sea fog away. As the horse plodded steadily along, he enjoyed the newly sunny day, the bird songs, and the light salt breeze. He passed the bridge that spanned the creek where his father had met his end. It brought back many memories, and a great deal of sadness. If his father had lived, could he have changed? Could they ever have had a meaningful part in each other's lives? Well there was no way to know, was there? It was too late and too long ago.

As he neared the midway point between Kirkwall and Stromness, the sky unexpectedly filled with threatening, fast-moving black clouds. Ty pulled the tarpaulin up over the contents of the wagon bed, and as the rain began to pelt him he tried to tug it over his head. The sun had disappeared and thunder growled and grumbled. Lightning skipped about, stabbing the ground with long flashing fingers. The road became a sea of mud. In the downpour, the Clydesdale started to lose his footing, and the wagon wheels slid in and out of the muddy tracks. A sudden bolt of lightning illuminated the silver coach coming toward them on the road and startled the horse harnessed to it. The animal reared up on its hind legs, startled. The coach lurched in the slippery mud and then suddenly toppled. Ty, who of course recognized it immediately, felt a chill of fright. Who was in it?

He jumped down from his wagon and ran toward the overturned carriage. At the edge of the road lay the coachman, a frail old fairy, muddy and short of breath. Ty started toward him, but he waved him away saying that he was all right, and he stood up to prove it. "Please," he pleaded, "see after my Lord!"

As Ty turned toward the coach, faint sounds led him to the figure of the fairy Earl, pinned beneath the side of the carriage. His chest was trapped under the weight of it. Ty fetched a board from the lift gate of his wagon and a rock from the side of the road. He positioned the board and stone to act as a lever and fulcrum. With his big strong body and sturdy arms he lifted the coach just enough to pull the old gentleman out of danger. Lord Fleming was breathing raggedly. His collarbone appeared to be broken, and there was a wide gash on his forehead caused by one of the spinning silver wheels. His fine clothes were covered with mud, and he was missing a shoe.

"Were you alone in there?" asked Ty, his heart in his throat. Lord Fleming nodded a weak yes. Relieved, Ty lifted him gently from the roadway and carried him to his wagon, where he settled him as comfortably as he could. "Wait here," he instructed the coachman. "I will send someone to help you."

He drove on down the road and turned into the lane leading to Lord Fleming's elegant home. The rain had stopped as suddenly as it had begun. Ty pulled the wagon up in the circular drive, shouting for help. Immediately the front door opened. Lady Fleming appeared first, followed by several servants. Ty led her to her husband, assuring her in a soothing tone that he was going to be alright.

He motioned for the servants to lift Lord Fleming from the wagon and carry him into the house. As they settled him onto the beautiful canopied bed in the master suite, Amelia came into the room, disturbed by the commotion. She was at once alarmed by the sight of her father and overjoyed at the sight of Ty.

After dispatching one of the servants to Kirkwall for the doctor and three more to recover the coachman, horse and carriage from the road, Ty began to explain to the family the events that had led to this moment. Mother and daughter listened as they loosened Lord Fleming's clothes and carefully washed the blood and grime from the wound on his forehead. When the doctor arrived, Ty politely excused himself, not wanting to intrude on the family's privacy. Amelia followed him to the door.

He felt that thistle down touch once again. "Dear Ty, how can we ever thank you for what you have done? After the awful way my father has treated you, you probably saved his life!"

"Every man's life is precious," answered Ty. "Your father's personal feelings toward me would never have hardened my heart toward him when he was in danger. And he is your father, after all."

He had acted instinctively to save this injured man, in spite of the painful insults that Lord Fleming had heaped on him. He could never have stood by without helping, and he knew that both he and Lord Fleming loved Amelia.

Ty searched her eyes, his own brimming with sincerity. The words suddenly began to pour out uncontrollably. "I must tell you, Amelia, that I love you. I think I have loved you from the first moment I saw you. Your father has made his opinion of me very clear, and I have honored his order to stay away from you. But every day I work as hard as I can to become someone worthy of you."

"I have built a thriving business with my sticky toffee pudding. I am confident that I will expand it to include more products. I have developed an international reputation."

"I did not expect to have a chance to tell you this, but I really wanted you to know about an honor that has come my way. I have been invited to participate in a dessert competition in Paris, France, sponsored by *La Chaine des Amateurs de Gateaux et Patisseries,* an organization of serious lovers of cakes and pastries."

"In order to register for the event, I had to supply a last name. So after some research and a lot of thought I have chosen what I believe is the perfect name for me.

Kelly. In Gaelic it means 'bright-headed.' I am confident enough to think the name applies in more ways than only to the color of my hair."

"I leave two days from now and will be back in three weeks. I will carry you in my heart, and I will win this competition in your honor. When I return, I hope to have news that you and your father have both made a complete recovery."

Ty stopped speaking, almost out of breath. This was the most personal of all the things he had ever said to Amelia. He was afraid he might have frightened her. But again she rested her fingers lightly on his arm.

"I love you too, Tyson Kelly. You are so kind, so intelligent. I feel the goodness and joy in your heart whenever I am near you."

"I am carefully sheltered by my parents. They believe they are doing the best thing for me, but I have my own mind. I will make my feelings clear to them, and my mother might very well support me."

"I will think of you with pride while you are in Paris. Meanwhile I'll stay close to my father and care for him. He is not a cruel person. He is just accustomed to making all the family decisions based on certain traditions. I believe your actions today will soften my father's heart when he reflects upon your selflessness. If you were not Ty you might not have helped him, but you are so very much who you are."

"My dear Ty, please take this with you to Paris as a reminder of my feelings for you." She pressed into his hand her delicate lace handkerchief. "Maybe it will bring you an extra bit of luck in the competition."

He tucked it gently into his breast pocket and smiled at her with his great big joyous smile. "I'll bring home the trophy."

Chapter Eight

Trip To Paris

The next two days Ty spent working, studying about Paris at the library, and packing. He was very excited to have the chance to visit that famous city, but he was nervous, too. He was going to have so many new and unfamiliar experiences. Ferries and trains would take him across Scotland and England, over the English Channel and on to Paris, the City of Light. As he boarded the ferry in Stromness and watched the port grow smaller he knew he was about to enter a brand new world.

He was surprised and a little frightened at the size of Paris. The beautiful buildings, wide avenues, delicate ironwork and green, flowering parks overwhelmed this boy who had grown up in a cave. The elegant Parisians with their stylish clothes made him conscious of his bulky, rough appearance and he wondered if he had made a mistake to come here. He really had to talk to himself to stay positive.

The night of the competition, he was so nervous that he arrived an hour early at its location, the world-famous restaurant *La Tour d'Argent*. The landmark building faced the River Seine, so he crossed the narrow street and leaned against the railing that extended along its bank. To his left he could see the back of Notre Dame cathedral on its island in the river, its graceful flying buttresses bathed in golden light and reflected in the water. If he had been himself he would have relished its beauty, but instead he was dizzy and lightheaded. His knees shook and his hands trembled. *Was it a mistake to come here?* he asked himself again.

He suddenly became aware of another young man, stylishly dressed in striped trousers, a finely tailored jacket, and a black top hat. He was standing a little further down the railing, looking at Ty. He smiled warmly. "Beautiful view, *n'est-ce pas*?"

"Incomparable!" replied Tyson, who actually did not have anything with which to compare it except St. Magnus cathedral at home.

"Are you here to see the competition?" the young man inquired.

"No, I am a competitor."

"And what is your specialty, monsieur?"

"Sticky Toffee Pudding. Yes indeed," Ty's voice quivered and he clasped his hands behind his back so that the fellow wouldn't see them shaking. They chatted a while longer about Paris, the competition, and the weather, until it was time to go in.

"I wish you the very best of luck! I sincerely hope you win." The fellow tipped his hat, smiled again and extended a hand of friendship as they began to move inside the building. Ty lost sight of him just after they reached the lobby.

As he walked toward the restaurant kitchen where the competition would take place, he concentrated his thoughts on Amelia and suddenly felt stronger. This was a once-in-a-lifetime chance for him. He had promised her he would win, so it was time to pull himself together.

The large commercial kitchen was equipped with enameled cast iron stoves. On the prep tables, burnished copper pots and pans awaited each contender, along with the ingredients required for his specialty. Ty checked his inventory carefully. Butter, dates, brown sugar, eggs, oranges. Check. Heavy cream, sugar, vanilla. Check. Curious about the competition, he looked about the kitchen. There were three other prep tables, each set like Ty's with the required cooking utensils and ingredients. As he watched, the other competitors claimed their positions and checked their ingredients as he had done. The five judges, all certified and highly respected, sat at a table in front of all of them. Spectators sat in rows of chairs along the back wall of the large kitchen.

The presiding judge, Monsieur Jolie, began to speak, and Ty turned to concentrate completely on his words. First the judge welcomed everyone, gave some background on the Society, thanked the restaurant owners for their sponsorship, introduced the other judges, and then addressed the contenders. "Gentlemen, welcome to Paris. You four have been carefully chosen from a large field of possible candidates because of your unique preparation of your specialty."

"From Holland we welcome Meneer Martyn Bakker, from Austria, Herr Manfred Adler, from France, Monsieur Marc Beaumont, and from Scotland, Mr. Tyson Kelly. You have been supplied with your necessary ingredients and preparation table as well as access to a restaurant stove. You will be judged on the taste of your dish, the originality of your recipe, and the uniqueness of your presentation. You will have one and a half hours to complete your assignment. Please begin now."

Ty's stomach fluttered at first, but he soon fell into the familiar rhythm of preparation. He planned to serve his pudding in individual ramekins rather than in one large dish so that his presentation would be unique. The hour and a half passed while all the participants concentrated on their cooking. At last, the presiding judge called time.

"Please place a portion of your completed entry in front of each judge," directed Monsieur Jolie. Ty topped each of his ramekins with a Scottish flag made of fondant and mounted on a hatpin, then joined the other contestants in delivering servings to the seated judges. After that, they all stepped back and waited, quiet and hopeful.

The judges sampled and made notes, speaking in low tones among themselves. One judge smiled and nodded as he sampled Meneer Bakker's crisp *banketletter*, or lettercake, filled with sweet almond paste. Others licked their lips over Herr Adler's *Sachertorte*, chocolate cake with raspberry jam spread between the layers. Monsieur Beaumont's *Mont Blanc*, a rich concoction of meringue, nuts, dark chocolate, chestnuts, and caramel, was apparently a delicious success as well. Ty began to believe the *Mont Blanc* would take first place, but they seemed to enjoy his pudding as well, so he held on to hope.

The judges continued to sample each delicious entry, making notes and murmuring quietly to each other. Ty carefully watched their reactions to the *Mont Blanc*. So many smiles and nods. He decided he was most likely sunk. No trophy to take home to Amelia.

Final scores were totaled. The presiding judge stood. "Gentlemen, you have each presented an outstanding entry in this competition. It has been extremely difficult to rank the winners because you are really all winners, champions in your craft. I am proud to announce that the third place award goes to Meneer Martyn Bakker of Holland. In second place is Monsieur Marc Beaumont of France. And"—here the judge paused dramatically—"the first place trophy goes to...Mr. Tyson Kelly, for his unparalleled rendition of sticky toffee pudding. None of us remember ever having had this dish more exquisitely conceived, prepared or presented. Congratulations, Mr. Kelly. Scotland will be proud of you."

Ty could scarcely believe it. He stood in amazement as the trophy was presented to him and the judges and other contestants crowded around to congratulate him. To think he had started in a cave and had now represent- ed his country and won a first place trophy. He blushed with embarrassment at the attention and with happi- ness at the cause of it.

The next morning, flush with victory, he went down to breakfast in the Montmartre *pensione*, the guest house where he had rented a room for the duration of his stay in Paris. He had chosen Montmartre because of his in- tense interest in art. Many artists lived and had studios in this colorful and bohemian section of Paris. Painters set up their easels in the squares and people chatted over coffee at small tables in the sun. He made his way to the ones on the sidewalk near a hedge of boxwoods.

The day was so beautiful. It was a joy to be having breakfast outside in the bright morning sun. "*Monsieur Kelly, bonjour!*" someone called out. It startled him, for he knew no one in Paris that he could think of, and he was still getting used to having a last name.

The handsome young man from the previous evening was rapidly approaching Ty's table.

"Congratulations on your spectacular victory last evening, Monsieur. May I join you? We didn't introduce ourselves last night. My name is Degas. Edgar Degas." Delighted to see him again, Ty nodded toward the oth- er chair, his eyes sparkling and his hair flaming in the sun. Monsieur Degas seemed sincerely glad to see him again—no odd looks, just a friendly smile. In the course of several *cafes au lait* and *croissants* he learned that the young man had been invited to last night's competition by the presiding judge, a close friend of the family. Young Degas was a native Parisian, the son of a successful banker. His father wanted him to study law, but Edgar had resisted. He was sure that his life's calling lay in painting. He had recently been studying in Italy and was now home again. Ty found him quite interesting and wanted to see some of his work, but did not know whether he should ask.

Suddenly Edgar inquired, "How much longer will you be in Paris, Monsieur?"

"I leave for home day after tomorrow," replied Ty. "I have been away too long."

"Well, I would truly like to have a taste of your prize-winning pudding. May I invite you to my home this evening? I'll include some of my friends. We'll cook a good Parisian dinner if you will make dessert. Maybe you would be interested in seeing some of my work. I am in the middle of several large portrait commissions."

Ty couldn't believe it! He was actually invited into this young Frenchman's home. He happily accepted the invitation and promised to be at the address supplied by his new friend promptly at nine o'clock.

It was a wonderful evening! He was quickly on a first name basis with Edgar and his friends and fellow artists Claude Monet, Pierre-Auguste Renoir, and Camille Pissarro. They were warm and friendly, and their energy filled the room. Like Edgar, they didn't seem aware that he was a troll, or if they were, they didn't care. Each had brought one of his own paintings for viewing and critique by the others. Ty soon understood that they did this on a regular basis. The constructive comments and discussion were fascinating to Ty, who knew and loved art and was now, through these painters, seeing it move in a new direction, with bright colors and loose brush-strokes. Their common idea was that a painting should be more an impression of a subject than a detailed, re-alistic image. Ty was consumed with curiosity about this new movement he learned was actually called "Impressionism" and peppered them with questions.

They were warmed by his enthusiasm and greatly impressed by his knowledge of art in general. He shyly mentioned that he painted in oils as well, which elicit-ed great interest and encouragement from all of them. They asked about his subject matter and equipment and offered him their special brushes and favorite tubes of paint for his own use. Their generosity was overwhelm-ing and very affirming.

After he heard their various life stories, he told them his. Everyone was amazed by how he had started out in a cave and wound up in Paris. The highlight of the lively meal was the sticky toffee pudding. Ty had prepared it expertly as he had the night before.

But, like all good things, the wonderful evening had to come to an end. They had talked for hours! It was quite late and time to leave. He reluctantly said good night to his new friends with the promise that he would stay in touch with them and hopefully return to Paris soon.

As Ty reached the door, Edgar invited him to join him at the Louvre the next day. Ty had planned to go by himself, but to visit that world-class museum with a real artist was a unique opportunity. Ty was surprised and pleased that Edgar found him good enough company to desire spend a whole day with him. He readily accepted the invitation. They planned to meet for breakfast in the morning.

The following day with Edgar was one of the most thrilling of Ty's life. The troll and the young gentleman strolled companionably through the great museum. Ty got goosebumps when he saw paintings and sculptures that he had studied in books. Their discussion of the art was full of personal conversation, as well. Edgar was particularly interested in the story of Ty and Amelia. As a portrait painter, he was fascinated with Ty's description of her gossamer wings, her gold-struck curls and her heavenly blue eyes. Ty promised to try to get a photograph of her so that Edgar could truly appreciate her beauty. He left Paris with a trophy and fast new friendships, especially with the young artist Degas.

Now he was on the ferry watching Stromness grow larger on the horizon. In his hands was the engraved gold trophy. As the ferry neared the dock, he wondered what lay in store for him.

Chapter Nine

Lord & Lady
Fleming
request the company of
Mr. Tyson Kelly
at dinner
Tuesday, the thirtieth of April at eight o'clock in the evening
R.s.v.p. Langbigging, Binscarth Road

A Formal
Invitation

When Ty arrived in Kirkwall, he went straight to his room at the Snooty Goose to unpack his clothes. Tacked to his door were two pieces of paper.

One was a copy of *The Orcadian*, the local weekly newspaper. It featured the story of his victory in Paris on the front page. Ty was surprised that the competition had drawn such interest in Kirkwall, let alone received a write-up in *The Orcadian*.

In such a close community as Kirkwall, the locals took great pride in each other's accomplishments. The annual flower show at St. Magnus produced numerous entries and great suspense until the winner's name was published on the front page of the paper. Local crafts, such as quilting, embroidery and jam-and-jelly-making received loyal coverage. Fishing and athletics attracted a lot of support. But Ty, to his knowledge, was the first to appear on the cover as an international competition winner—at the very least the first troll to do it. He allowed himself a moment of pleasure.

The other paper was a personal note from Mr. Higbee. It read, "Congratulations, Ty. We are very proud of you. Please come to see me as soon as you can. I have a message for you."

What possible message could he have? wondered Ty as he tried to keep his mind from racing.

Rather than prolong the suspense, he went straight down to the office and greeted Mr. Higbee. After a warm hug and hearty congratulations, his friend handed him an ivory envelope, handed him an ivory envelope. His name was written on it in exquisite calligraphy, "Mr. Tyson Kelly." With his heart in his throat, he opened the envelope and read:

Lord and Lady Fleming
request the company
of
Mr. Tyson Kelly
at dinner
Tuesday, the 30th of April
eight o'clock in the evening
r.s.v.p. Langbigging, Binscarth Road

Ty could hardly collect his thoughts. He was invited to the Flemings' home for dinner! How could it be? Lord Fleming had always been perfectly clear about his opinion of him. He dared not be too hopeful.

So, first things first. He wrote a note of acceptance on Snooty Goose paper, reminding himself that he needed to see about some proper stationery of his own. Then he checked his modest wardrobe. He had a fine new suit, thanks to his trip to Paris. He carefully brushed it so that it would be presentable for the evening with Amelia's parents. Then he went down the street to post the note. It was now the twenty-eighth of April, so he comforted himself that he had only two days, too short a time to become overly nervous. He plunged himself immediately into work, but thoughts about the upcoming evening kept interrupting his concentration.

Lord Fleming, in the days that he lay in bed recuperating from his accident, had a lot to consider. He had opposed Tyson so completely and, in his mind, so rightly. His intelligent, beautiful daughter should have a wonderful future ahead of her. And yet, when he visited her future, the troll was there! If he continued to object, would it do more harm than good? Was it possible that he was misjudging Tyson? Was he stubbornly closing his eyes to facts that were undeniable? He had done everything he could to drive the troll away, and yet Amelia's affection for him was constant. She had asked for him during her illness.

And when he, Lord Fleming, was injured in the carriage accident, what did the troll do? He came straight to help him. If Lord Fleming were entirely honest with himself, Tyson had probably saved his life. If he had lain out there in the rain, injured and bleeding, he could have developed pneumonia. At his age, he might not have survived that.

During his days of healing, Amelia tended to him, changing his bandages and feeding him nourishing dishes prepared by the cook. Each day, she remarked about Tyson's unselfish act and her gratitude that he had saved her father's life. Whenever she mentioned him, her expression grew soft and her eyes pleaded for Lord Fleming's understanding. His unbending attitude finally began to soften in response until over the stretch of weeks his stubborn convictions began to change. He gradually became more and more ashamed as he faced the truth and admitted to himself that he had been wrong! Blind pride was the culprit. He had puffed himself up with pride. He believed he and his fairy clan were superior to any other race and he thought nothing of making that clear, even if it hurt someone. Why did he believe that? Well, he had been taught to believe that. But was he right? Had he trusted bigoted judgment without considering that it might be flawed? Where had he gotten his low opinion about the intelligence and worthiness of trolls? He'd always had that opinion. Everyone he knew had the same opinion. But had he ever known any trolls? Well, honestly, only one. This one. And this one deserved respect and admiration. His daughter had finally brought him to see Ty through her eyes, and Lord Fleming knew that she was the one with clear judgment. Humbled and shaken, he came to accept what had once been impossible for him to face. Ty was in his daughter's future. Lord Fleming had seen him there, and he had every right to be there.

Lord Fleming wanted to share his change of heart with his wife, and he knew he had to confess the secret he had kept from her. He found her reading in the parlor and took her hand, lifting her from her chair. She regarded him with curiosity. "My dear," he began, "I kept something from you when I returned from my time travel trip during Amelia's illness. I saw the troll there in the future with her. I didn't tell you because I just couldn't accept it. But, as you know, I have been wrestling with myself over this, and I can finally admit that I have been wrong. I am ashamed of my behavior toward him and toward Amelia. I am ashamed of having kept something from you that I should have shared. Can you ever forgive me?"

Cupping his troubled face gently between her hands Lady Fleming replied, "I have kept something from you as well. While you were on that very trip I brought Ty inside the house and to Amelia's bedside. The sound of his voice was the beginning of her recovery. I am not sorry for what I did, but I have been burdened by the secret. Can you forgive me for not telling you?"

Lord Fleming was silent for a moment, coming to terms with her words. Then he assured her. "You did the right thing, dear. It was the only answer. I am just sorry that my behavior compelled you to keep silent. From now on we shall keep no more secrets from each other, agreed?"

They held each other tightly, relief flooding both of them. They had loved each other a long time, and confession is good for the soul.

Chapter Ten

Anticipation

His suit was pressed and his shoes polished. As Tyson peered into the mirror over his dresser, his appearance suddenly concerned him. He tried to tame his unruly red hair with oil with little success. He decided that it was a futile effort. Perhaps he should accept his hair in its natural state, since no one else, including Amelia, had ever seen him otherwise. Maybe he should just be himself. That was probably best. He straightened his tie, smoothed his freshly starched shirt and put on his jacket. As he examined himself once again in his dresser mirror, he thought he actually looked quite presentable, or at the very least, quite distinctive. He knew that he was as ready as he would ever be. Taking a deep breath, Ty walked out the door. His heart hammered in his chest as he hitched the horse to the wagon.

There were just so many ifs to consider. If the evening was going to be a success or a disaster. If Lord Fleming had reconsidered his attitude toward Ty. If only he weren't a troll. He had never been so nervous. Not even his trip to Paris and the competition could compare to the importance of this evening. He was trembling with anticipation and anxiety. His thoughts looped over and over again as he drove his wagon to Binscarth Road. Self-doubts surfaced and began to chip away at his confidence, yet he became strangely calm when he thought of Amelia. *Yes!* he told himself. *Yes, I can do this! I will just be myself to Lord Fleming. The self his daughter loves. It may take time, but he will eventually realize he doesn't have to protect her from the most sincere love she will ever be offered.*

Ty's jaw sagged slightly as he passed through the stone pillared entry and cast-iron gates at the Fleming mansion. Large over-hanging trees framed the house, and meticulously trimmed hedges flanked the driveway.

His rented wagon and horse seemed so out of place in such a formal setting. As he was looping the horse's reins around the cast iron hitching post, he made a decision. He was going to buy this magnificent Clydesdale that had served him so well on the many trips between Kirkwall and Stromness. *Yes, and I'll buy the wagon too!* His jaw tightened once again with determination. As he approached the steps to the front door, he was struck with yet another idea, the name for his future company: Great Scot Sweets. Then he climbed the steps and rapped the exquisitely detailed silver knocker. He paused, holding his breath. His future would soon reveal itself, just on the other side of this magnificently carved door.

Chapter Eleven

Beyond All Expectations

The great mahogany door swung open. A uniformed servant invited Ty inside and announced his arrival, and Lord and Lady Fleming appeared in the great hall followed by Amelia. Had Tyson not just spent time in Paris, he would have been overwhelmed by the grandness of the elegant home with its warm wood paneling, crystal chandeliers, velvet and silk draperies and stylishly upholstered furniture. The Flemings were as splendidly dressed as their home, but before Ty could become self-conscious again, his eye caught Amelia's and she smiled such a warm smile that he could have easily forgotten where he was.

Lord Fleming stepped forward, his recent wounds unnoticeable except for a crimson scar on his forehead.

He extended his hand to Ty. "Welcome to our home, Mr. Kelly. I owe you a great debt of gratitude. You saved my life on the road, and in doing so you showed your true character. My daughter recognized your kind and generous heart while I was judging your origins. She was right, and I was wrong. I hope you will accept my most sincere apology." Ty's eyes widened in surprise and he was speechless for a moment. Amelia moved to her father's side, kissed his cheek and squeezed his hand in approval. Lady Fleming's face relaxed with relief. Ty spoke, "Sir, I know that you have always acted in your daughter's best interest. I fully understand that, and I would expect no less of you. I appreciate the invitation to your home this evening. I am grateful for the opportunity to know you and your family better. I hope that as you come to know me, you will see me as a responsible and dependable person." He smiled his wonderful smile.

The serious beginning to the evening behind them, they sipped sherry and chatted about the weather and local news before dinner. Tyson began to relax a little. Each time he glanced at Amelia, he felt like pinching himself to be sure that he was actually in the Flemings' home. After a time, the butler entered the room to announce that dinner was served.

During the sumptuous meal, elegantly served in the glow of many candles and reflected in abundant crystal and silver, Ty briefly recounted the story of his adventures in Paris. He spoke modestly about his victory in the competition, but Lord Fleming pressed him for details, and before he knew it, Ty was telling him about his plans to expand his sticky toffee pudding business to include other confections such as scones and rich, delicious cakes. At Hogmanay, he envisioned special gingerbread house creations complete with transparent sugar windows tinted like leaded glass, window boxes and roofs shingled with gumdrops, his favorite candy. As he talked, he realized that he was describing confectionery versions of the home he wanted to build, and his animated description completely captured Lord Fleming's imagination. "Oh my, yes," he exclaimed.

"Not only restaurants but fine hotels will be quite interested in permanent orders for your products. I shall contact my hotel managers if you wish, and have them contact you right away."

For the second time that evening, Ty was momentarily speechless. He had no idea what Lord Fleming might be speaking of, because he knew nothing about him really, except that he had apparently been a successful businessman. "Sir, I'm sorry. I don't understand. What do you mean?" "Well, before I retired to Orkney, I headed a worldwide group of luxury hotels. At my age, I wanted to retire to spend more time with my family, so I gave up my leadership position but I still own the hotels. I know a lot about hotel dining rooms of course, and I know that a steady source of quality products is most important to their success. Your idea about the gingerbread houses fascinates me. Not only will they serve as decorations in the dining rooms but also in the lobbies at Hogmanay.

Whole families will come to our Scottish hotels to see them, and hotels in other countries may adapt them to their own holiday celebrations. I am very interested in speaking further with you about this, but not now. I'm sure the ladies and I would like to hear more about your trip to the continent."

Ty's mind was spinning, but he gathered his thoughts and was soon describing ferries and trains and the beautiful avenues and buildings of Paris. He told them about the friendship he formed with the young artists, especially with Edgar Degas and described their new, fresh method of painting.

"I'm sure we will all hear of them. They will be famous, I'm certain. Their technique is an important departure from the painting styles we are used to seeing. Edgar and I visited the Louvre together for a day. I think it is the most important museum in the world, and someday the paintings of these extraordinary artists will be hanging there beside the Old Masters." Amelia expressed particular interest in this description of the new art and the artists, and it gave Ty courage enough to ask, "Have you ever been photographed? Monsieur Degas was enchanted by my description of you. I promised that if I could obtain a photo of you, I would send it to him. He would return it, of course. I think once he sees your photograph, he will want to paint your portrait." Lord Fleming broke in to say that a studio photograph had been taken of Amelia earlier in the year and there was a small copy of it. "You have described Monsieur Degas as a sensible young man, well brought up and remarkably talented. You may send the photograph to him."

After dinner, Lord Fleming handed him the small picture, and he tucked it safely into his pocket. Amelia accompanied him to the door, and as she touched his arm once again as lightly as thistle down, another thought bloomed in his head. That would be the name of his home. Thistle Downe. How absolutely perfect! He smiled his big smile and took his leave, walking on air.

Chapter Twelve

Great Scot
Sweets

In the days that followed the dinner, Lord Fleming conferred with Ty several times about his business plans. Ty needed a factory space where he could prepare his greatly expanded line of confections. He needed many more wagons and horses. Remembering his inspiration while standing on the Fleming steps, he named his company Great Scot Sweets and started to advertise for new employees. He explored available real estate in Stromness and found a building with a large commercial kitchen. More horses were easy to come by, and he rented a nearby stable. Wagons he could store behind his building. Mr. Higbee let him conduct employee interviews in the back room of the Snooty Goose.

Lord Fleming had followed up with his hotel managers and orders were beginning to come in.

Production got underway. Ty could see that his business was going to be quite successful, and he decided to return to the Higbees the share of the Snooty Goose they had given to him so they could sell the pub at a fine profit and retire in their old age.

Every day he thought of Amelia and saw her as often as he could. He took time as well to make some decisions about the home he planned to build. He got a letter off to Edgar, telling him of the latest developments and enclosing the photograph and kept his promise to Amelia by making an appointment for them to visit Miss McNamara. She was delighted that Amelia wanted to take her place as schoolteacher, and Amelia couldn't stop smiling.

One afternoon, he slipped away quietly and chose a home site in The Wood, a small forested area between Kirkwall and Stromness. Now he could begin Thistle Downe. He went back to his room at the Snooty Goose and started to sketch his ideas. In his mind's eye he could see the home—a two-storied house built of wood imported from mainland Scotland instead of stones from the local fields, unusual for Orkney. It would be spacious but welcoming, warmed by a great stone fireplace in the heart of it. His conversations with his artist friends in Paris had made him aware of the importance of light and its effects. He wanted beautiful natural light throughout, which called for many large windows. He would have to find the best craftsmen available, so he started a list of the experts he would need. He needed woodworkers for the millwork and the finest glaziers for the windows; he needed skilled carpenters for both outside and inside construction and stoneworkers for the entry and the terrace and, of course, for his long anticipated fireplace. He would need furniture builders and upholsterers and advice on the kitchen. And landscapers. He filled sheet after sheet of paper with drawings and specifications. With each pen stroke, the house became more real to him. His dreams were, to his amazement, beginning to approach reality.

Ty was becoming a frequent guest in the Fleming home. Lord Fleming had taken quite a liking to him and enjoyed his sunny disposition and his sense of humor. He also admired his work ethic, which was strong and focused.

Lady Fleming already regarded him highly and now she had become extremely fond of him as well. She often asked his opinion on local events. They walked in the home's lovely gardens; she acquainted him with the names of the flowers and shrubs. Drawing on his life in the country, Ty shared his observations about the wild versus the cultivated plants. One day, she greeted him with a kiss on each cheek. Ty was silently deeply moved. For the second time in his life, he felt the warmth of motherly affection. He would have missed so much if he hadn't had Mrs. Higbee to love him, and suddenly now more than anything, he wanted to take Amelia home to meet her. Mrs. Higbee was thrilled and excited and bubbled happily into action. Sunday night a week later, the four of them were enjoying an animated conversation full of laughter over supper at the Snooty Goose. Amelia loved them right away. It was easy to see why the Higbees had been so important to Ty's happiness. They in turn felt immediately at ease with this enchanting fairy. Her gentle spirit and easy manner drew them close. Ty smiled all evening. It was all going to be okay.

Chapter Thirteen

An Unexpected Applicant

As months passed and the Hogmanay celebration approached, Great Scot Sweets was flooded with orders. There were many hotels in Lord Fleming's group. Once other hotels and restaurants saw the gingerbread houses and realized the potential attraction for customers, they began to order as well. Ty and his employees were working around the clock baking the festive houses with their jewel-colored windows, their sloped roofs shingled with gumdrops and icicles made of spun sugar hanging from their eaves. Orders were coming in from all over Scotland. The horses were so busy coming and going that it was hard to take them out of commission long enough to have their iron shoes replaced by a general farrier. His stable manager suggested they hire a full time farrier of their own. So a sign went up in the factory's front window.

A week later, Ty was at his desk working on his books when the manager knocked. "We have an applicant for the farrier position. Do you have time to see him now?" "Of course," answered Ty. "Send him in." He looked back at the figures he was adding up in his ledger. In a moment, he glanced up at the doorway again, expecting the applicant. A dark shape filled it, blocking the sunlight. A gnarled, twisted shape. A shape from his childhood, forever seared into his memory! Shock and disbelief flooded him. He couldn't move; his throat shut tight with a fierce spasm of pain. Blood rushed to his head. He felt suddenly dizzy, as if he had floated to the ceiling of the room. The misshapen figure began to move toward his desk, shuffling, eyes on the floor.

Ty finally found his voice. "Father!" he shouted. Gareth stopped and looked up in fright and confusion. Their eyes locked with lightning recognition. "How could this happen, father? How can you be here? I thought you had drowned. I thought you were dead all these years! Where have you been? How have you been living?"

Gareth sank to the floor. He looked ancient, ragged and worn. Finally, he began to speak. "After the goats knocked me into the water, and I went over the waterfall, the current swept me down to the coast. I had nothing but the clothes on my back. But the fact that I didn't drown made me realize that I had a second chance at life. A chance to mend my ways and be more like the person your mother had loved. I made up my mind to give up robbery and live an honest life. If I could do it, I would then try to find you and be the father I should have been, or if too much time had passed, at least be your friend. I never told you how your mother died. It was in giving birth to you. I blamed you for her death and I couldn't let myself love you. I was so wretchedly wrong. You were a little baby. Your mother wanted you so much, and we three would have been a happy family, I'm sure. But my heart was too damaged to make room for you. Over these years, I have worked odd jobs, some farrier work and some carpentry. People have been kind enough to give me shelter in their barns and sheds and food from their tables."

"How did you come to Kirkwall?"

"Just followed the road. I got as far as our cave, but of course you were long gone. I knew that you would have taken care of yourself. You had inherited your mother's cheerful disposition and resourcefulness." He paused and brushed his shaggy hair from his eyes. "I'm sorry I didn't love you as I should have, Tyson. I was just a simple-minded troll. So I kept moving, surviving, growing older and more regretful, always hoping to find you and tell you I'm sorry for my lack of affection towards you, and for the terrible example I set for you."

"But when did you arrive in Kirkwall?"

"Just last night. I cleaned up at the brook this morning and started out to find work. I knocked on doors, asking if anyone had odd jobs for me or if someone's horses needed shoeing. At a house down the street a fellow told me this business was looking for a farrier. I thought it was my lucky day! How would I have ever guessed that you were here and this place belonged to you?"

"My name is on the sign in front in big letters, Father. Tyson. Didn't you see it? You wouldn't have recognized Kelly; I chose that myself."

Gareth sighed and lowered his head. "Tyson, don't you remember that I cannot read?"

With that, Ty's heart melted. He had made such a success of his life that he had temporarily forgotten his simple beginnings.

He had taken for granted the gift of his education, the support of the Higbees, Miss McNamara and other friends who had helped him become a useful citizen. His father had remained illiterate, struggling to survive each day by performing odd jobs and living hand to mouth. But Gareth had made a real effort to change his ways, and Ty saw that his redemption was possible. What could he do? He never even thought of his father any more. But could he turn him away? His mind churned, and then the only right answer rose to the top. He remembered the day so long ago that he was told of Gareth's supposed drowning. He had regretted not having said or done something kind for his father that morning. Miraculously, he now had a second chance. He gently took Gareth's hand and helped him up from the floor. He put his arm around him and led him to a chair. "Your journey is over, father. You can stay here with me. Your skills as a farrier are sorely needed in my company. You will have a roof over your head and plenty to eat. It's not too late for you to once more be the man my mother loved. So now let me take you to the place where I live. You can have a bath, and I'll find some fresh clothes for you. My friends the Higbees will feed you a hearty meal." Gareth stared at his long-lost son and tears coursed down his rough, lined face, blinding him with relief and gratitude. Somehow his son, who had received nothing good from him, had the heart to forgive him! Those long, lonely years would be behind him. He was old and frail, but suddenly his heart felt alive, and seeds of love so long dormant began to sprout in it. Ty helped his father into the wagon and drove him to the Snooty Goose. "We'll get you bathed and dressed. You'll feel better after that. Then you will meet my dear friends, the Higbees. They have taken care of me since I was fifteen years old. They gave me a job; they helped me go to school. It was in their kitchen that I learned to make my famous sticky toffee pudding. They encouraged me to start my own business. They have been like my family. Let's go to them now."

The Higbees were surprised and alarmed when they saw Ty enter the front door, closely followed by a giant, looming troll they had never seen before. Was Ty in danger? Had this menacing stranger taken him hostage with the intent to rob the pub? Mr. Higbee took a step forward, uncertain about what he would do but instinctively protective of Ty. Ty held up his hand, signaling him to stop.

"My dear friends, all is well. Don't be afraid. I have news that will shock you, and rightly so. I am still shaken myself about what has happened today. This is my father, Gareth, whom I thought drowned years ago. He showed up in Kirkwall last night and applied for the farrier job at Great Scot Sweets today. He had no idea that I lived here or that the business belonged to me. When we saw each other, we were both stunned and astonished." He took Gareth's arm and encouraged him to move forward. "We have had a long talk about what has happened over the years since our separation. He told me that when he survived his near drowning, he made up his mind to try to start over and change his ways. He has been working odd jobs all these years, wandering, accepting food and shelter when it was offered. It has been a hard and lonely time for him, but he has stuck to his resolution to remain honest. He has apologized to me and I believe that he is sincere. I have told him all about you. I hope that you can accept him as I have."

After a few moments of silence, Mrs. Higbee spoke. "Ty, we love you. If you can accept him in your life, then of course we accept him, too." Mr. Higbee nodded in agreement. "Thank you," Gareth spoke, his voice thick with emotion. "You have loved Tyson as I should have. I have no right to expect anything from any of you but I am very grateful. I'll do everything I can to prove to you that I have changed." Ty broke in, smiling at the Higbees. "I am grateful to you, too. We will start anew as of today." "Well, then," Mrs. Higbee asked, "Who's hungry? It's time for lunch!"

After Gareth had filled his empty stomach, Ty took him back to the factory and installed him in the back room where he could rest. Then, he went to give the Flemings the shocking news that his father was alive and in fact in Kirkwall. How would they take it? His whole life could turn upside down because of this. It had taken a long time for Lord Fleming to accept him. How would he react to his father? Ty felt the old quivering in his stomach that signaled a bout of self-doubt, but he told himself it had to be done.

Amelia saw his wagon pull up in front of the house and knew as soon as she saw him that he was unnerved and upset. Before he even had time to knock, she flung open the door and rushed to him. His face, usually ruddy, was grey. The pain she saw in his eyes made her heart ache. "I have some staggering news," Ty whispered to her. "My father is alive and here in Kirkwall. It is a long, strange story, and one I have to tell your parents now while I have the strength to do it." Amelia grew pale with alarm. It had all been going so well. Would this new development upset everything? "My father is not at home, Ty. He won't be back until tomorrow. But mother is here. Could you tell the two of us?"

Ty studied her anxious face. "Yes, Amelia, I will. It wouldn't be fair to keep you in suspense. Call your mother, please." The tone of her daughter's voice made Lady Fleming hurry into the room. "Mother, Ty has something to tell us. It will shock you, but please hear him out." Her legs were beginning to tremble. "Can we sit down first?" Ty sank gratefully into a chair. He began to relate the events of the day. They were dismayed at first. They knew of Ty's difficult relationship with his father. They were surprised to learn that he had not drowned and amazed that he had showed up like a ghost from the past at Ty's workplace. They were suspicious of his intention to reform his life, but Ty assured them that he believed it was a genuine effort. Had they not known Ty so well they would have been astonished that he had made such a quick decision to accept his father. They were concerned, as Ty was, about how Lord Fleming would accept this news about Ty's criminal troll father living in Kirkwall with him.

Ty finished talking, and all three sat quietly, absorbing the unsettling turn of events. Lady Fleming finally spoke.

"Ty, I have to say, I admire your ability to forgive your father so quickly. But his presence here may complicate things. As you have related to us, he spent most of his life involved in robbery and abusive behavior, and now he will be living with you in Kirkwall. Hopefully he has reformed, but we are not yet sure of that.

"My husband may have some difficulty with this. Adjusting to your father and his presence here may take some time. We don't really know much about him."

Amelia's small face crumpled in a torrent of tears. Ty pulled her lace handkerchief from its place in his breast pocket and dabbed at her cheek in a futile effort to help her. He didn't know what he could say that would comfort her, and her tears were tormenting him.

"I know that my new situation may be a problem, but I cannot turn my father away," his dark, troubled eyes begged her to understand. "I can only pray the soul-searching that led to your father's acceptance of me will extend to my father."

Amelia began to speak, her soft voice choked with tears. "Dear Ty, once again you are so true to yourself. Your compassion and generous spirit define you." She stood up, her voice rising and clearing until it filled the room. "You mean everything to me. I willingly accept your father because I trust your judgment." She paused, steeling herself for her next words. "I love my father. He has been devoted to me. I have never been more proud of him than when he swallowed his pride and allowed himself to see you as I do. He had the chance to change and he did it. Your father deserves the same chance. I have been so happy for the past few peaceful months and I cannot bear the thought of renewed turmoil. If this new development results in any attempt to separate us, I will stand firmly at your side, Ty, whatever the cost."

Her mother stared at Amelia, stunned at her words. *Whatever the cost.* Was she once again in danger of losing her only daughter? Would she once more be torn between her love for her husband and her love for her child? She buried her face in her hands.

"We need to give Lord Fleming a chance to hear the news," Ty reminded the two. "We don't know what he will think and we shouldn't try to guess. We will respect his need for time to process this development. I will wait to hear from him." He lifted Amelia's tiny hand to his lips. "We will be patient and trust in the changes in both our fathers."

He left the Fleming home greatly burdened. How could he leave Amelia in this state of confusion? Meanwhile, he knew he had to go see about Gareth, who was waiting alone in a strange place. He would be hungry again.

Turning his attention to his newly arrived father, he realized that Gareth was desperately in need of new clothes. Forcing himself to put his worries in a drawer for the moment, he loaded Gareth into the wagon and drove him down to McDuff's dry goods store. Word of his presence spread through town quickly, and opinions twittered up and down the street like wild birds. Some thought there was no reason for Ty to forgive his father; others knew his kind nature and great heart would not allow him to do otherwise. Gareth, aware of the attention and uncertain about what he should do, just kept his head down and followed his son.

In the oppressive darkness of his room that night, Ty tossed and turned until the bed was a tangle of damp sheets. There was no way he could stop loving Amelia, nor could he refuse to accept Gareth, who had made such an effort to redeem himself. He endured the next day, sure that by nightfall Lord Fleming would be aware of Gareth's presence. No word came that evening and there was silence all the following day. Ty thought his nerves would pop out of his skin. Through another endless, uneasy night, he tried to reassure himself that Amelia's father would be the man he thought he was. But why had he heard nothing? That troubled him.

In the morning, Mr. Higbee greeted him with a letter he said had just arrived via the silver carriage. It was addressed to Ty in Lord Fleming's bold handwriting. His heart started hammering so hard it shook his chest as he took the letter to his room and sat down to open it. It read:

Dear Ty,

My wife and daughter have told me of the appearance of your father in Kirkwall and in your life. I was delayed by a day before I was able to return from my trip. Otherwise, you would have heard from me sooner. I understand you all have been apprehensive about my reaction to this news. I am so very sorry for that. During my re-evaluation of my feelings about you, I slowly renounced the prejudices of a lifetime. I rejected my misplaced pride and the snobbery it generated in me. The change is permanent.

I understand that your father has committed to change his life. I know how hard a task that is,

*having done it myself. He deserves the chance
to succeed.*

*Please bring him to our home at three o'clock this
afternoon so that we may be introduced. We will
all be happy to see you.*

Sincerely,
Lord Magnus Fleming

Ty dropped his fiery head into his hands in a flood of
relief. This was not the old Lord Fleming. His words were
sincere evidence of his reformation. Ty felt enormous respect for the man's humility. He hurried over to the factory and helped Gareth dress in his brand new clothes–
neatly pressed dark trousers, crisp white shirt, striped
waistcoat, and shiny new leather shoes. He took him for
a haircut and shave at the local barber's. Gareth looked
decidedly better than when he arrived in Kirkwall.

On the drive to their home, Ty told his father in de-
tail about the Flemings and his love for Amelia. As he
talked, Gareth seemed to shrink inside his new clothes.
He realized that he could ruin his son's chance for happiness just by showing up in his life again. He was rough
and ignorant—nothing like these folks or even like his
son. As they climbed out of the wagon and approached
the Flemings' grand front door, Gareth's knees gave way,
so Ty slipped his arm around his waist to hold him up.
Ty rapped the knocker and Amelia herself opened the

door. Gareth's eyes were fixed on his shiny new shoes. He dared not look up. Then Amelia reached out and put her hand on his arm. He raised his eyes to meet hers, and she smiled the warmest, kindest smile. To his great surprise, he smiled back. It was his first smile in over twenty years. The tension in the room dissolved. Everything was going to be alright.

Chapter Fourteen

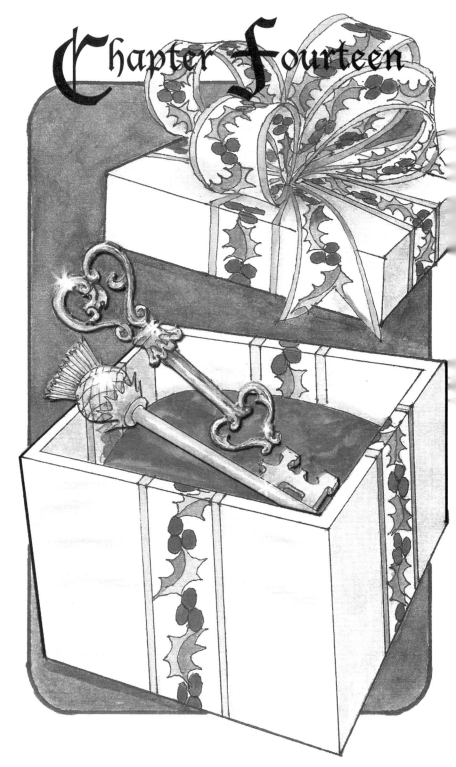

A Hogmanay Proposal

ogmanay evening, Ty and Gareth arrived at the Fleming home in time for dinner. They were greeted by great ceremonial torches at the front door, in keeping with the celebration. What a wonderful evening they had, laughing, talking, enjoying roast goose and tatties and sticky toffee pudding. Gareth couldn't stop smiling. Not since his life with Eva had he been in a house to celebrate Hogmanay. And not since her death had he celebrated the holiday at all. In the years he had been alone, he often regretted having denied Tyson that pleasure. Each lonely year, he stood outside in the shadows and gazed into windows of cottages where families and friends were gathered. He could not hear them; he could only see them and imagine their chatter and their merry laughter as they exchanged gifts. He watched them seated at table, where after a proper blessing they enjoyed a celebratory meal. Never was he invited into any of the homes, but then why should he be? He was dirty and ragged and ugly, and he had nothing to offer.

And now, this miracle had occurred. He had been given another chance at life. He vowed once again to himself to make good on it. Tears slipped silently down his wrinkled cheeks. Some were tears of regret, but most were tears of gratitude. He looked at his son, standing in front of the great fire crackling in the fireplace, radiating happiness and health. He felt the kindness and acceptance of the lovely girl who held his son's heart in her dainty hands. His own heart swelled with joy.

After dinner, Tyson asked Lord Fleming if he could speak to him in private. In the library, Ty came straight to the point. "Sir, you and your family have been very kind to me and now to my father. I have the greatest respect and affection for you and your wife. You know your daughter has been the light of my life since I first saw her. I have earnestly tried to prove to you that I can be worthy of her. I am asking for her hand in marriage. I can support her with worldly possessions. She will live in comfort at Thistle Downe, but more importantly I will stand beside her through all the good times as well as the bad, and I will love her with all my heart for the rest of my life."

Lord Fleming studied him for a long time, saying nothing. Ty's confidence began to waver slightly. Had he misjudged Amelia's parents' regard for him? Did Lord

Fleming still have reservations about him? His red hair drooped and his smile began to quiver slightly. Finally, Lord Fleming spoke.

"Tyson, as you remember, I had a very unkind opinion of you when I first saw you. I judged you strictly on your background and your appearance. But Amelia saw your great qualities from the beginning. She saw the kindness of your spirit and the sincerity in your heart. As I have told you I came to recognize those qualities too and admire your determination and your willingness to work. You have shown such great imagination and creativity in building a thriving business, but never do you ask an employee to do anything you are not willing to do yourself. You have shown your loyalty to your friends, the Higbees, who were kind enough to provide you with your first opportunity to improve your life. Lady Fleming and I would be proud to have you as part of our family. You have our blessing."

Tyson's face stretched into the widest, happiest smile ever, and they left the room arm in arm.

Work was progressing rapidly on Thistle Downe. Ty had contracted with all the necessary workmen, and the home was taking shape just as he had hoped it would. Walls were up, windows installed and the roof was in place. Now work could begin on the inside. The parlor was dominated by the massive stone fireplace of his dreams. Ty wanted to propose to Amelia at Thistle Downe because she and the home were the most cherished parts of his life. So in the days leading up to Hogmanay, in anticipation of Lord Fleming's blessing, he and Mrs. Higbee decorated the unfinished parlor with candles. They placed sprigs of holly by the door and along the mantel as a symbolic offering of shelter to small woodland creatures, as was the common practice. They planned a lovely dinner to be served January 1, the day after Hogmanay, in front of the great fireplace on a table set with embroidered linens and fresh flowers. It would be the beginning of a new year and perhaps a new life for Tyson and Amelia. Tyson placed an elegantly wrapped small package on the mantel. Then he called at the Fleming home for Amelia. She was delighted to go to Thistle Downe to see the progress, but she had no idea what lay in store for the evening. As they drew near the house, she exclaimed with pleasure at the beautiful windows with their leaded diamond-shaped panes and warm colors, and the smoke curling out of the chimney. Inside the house, she smiled at the sight of the table set so nicely. Ty escorted her to her chair, and Mrs. Higbee herself served their dinner.

The full moon was shining in the windows and the embers were glowing in the fireplace when Ty rose from his chair, took the little box from the fireplace mantel and placed it in front of Amelia.

"My dear Amelia, you know you are the center of my life. I believe the contents of this box will show you how deeply I care." With trembling fingers Amelia untied the ribbon and removed the lid. Inside were two keys, one large and one small. The large brass key was obviously the key to Thistle Downe. The smaller one was an exquisitely fashioned silver key on a delicate chain. She lifted it from the box to examine it more closely. "That," murmured Ty, "is the key to my heart. You will have it always." He took it from her hands and tenderly fastened it around her slender neck. "I have asked your father and mother for your hand and they have given me their blessing. Now I am asking you. Will you be my wife?"

Amelia's cheeks grew pink and her wings fluttered slightly; she lifted her chin and looked directly into Ty's earnest face. "Yes. Yes, Ty. I am honored by your proposal. You represent everything good and admirable, and you set an example for all to follow. I will be proud to be your wife."

Ty realized that he had been holding his breath, and he gasped and grinned at the same time, his heart swelling and his hair flaming. For a moment he could not believe his life, his great good fortune in overcoming his early existence and making a useful and successful place for himself in the world. And now to know that this sensitive, intelligent beauty saw such good in him almost brought him to his knees. "Then we will finish Thistle Downe together and plan a wonderful wedding, Amelia."

Chapter Fifteen

Thistle Downe

The couple took up the completion of Thistle Downe with enthusiasm, inspired now by the assurance that they would share their lives there. Amelia chose lovely antique laces for the bed and the bath, and for the dining room an ample table, large enough to seat their family and friends. They chose a sturdy cast-iron stove for the kitchen and a pot rack hung with glowing copper pots. There were lovely window boxes spilling over with flowers and a covered double swing where they could enjoy the summer breezes and read or dream. In the parlor, there was cozy seating in front of the fire and many books.

They invited Gareth to live with them in their home, but he quickly declined. He was comfortable in his room in the factory, and by living there he could serve as night watchman, which added to his feeling of usefulness. It was good for Gareth to be needed and appreciated. He felt accepted by Ty's friends and his family-to-be, and so very grateful and humbled for all the recent changes in his life.

As the days passed, he had been able to slowly relax the emotional cap on his memories enough to share more about Eva with Ty. That had been healing for both of them. Ty had taken him to visit Miss McNamara with a special request in mind. Gareth sat, head down, his rough hands resting on the knees of his blue workpants, as his son spoke.

"Miss McNamara, you are a gifted teacher. You have educated and inspired so many children during your life, including me. Now that you are retiring, I want to ask you to try something new. Would you teach my father to read?"

Miss McNamara, who had been a little uncertain about how to fill her days after she left the school, adjusted her glasses and began to smile. Over the years, she had lost both parents, so the house was empty and she was alone. Teaching Gareth would occupy some of her time.

"Of course I will! It would be a pleasure," she assented. Gareth, feeling that he should offer something in exchange, told her that he was a pretty good carpenter and would gladly make himself available to her for jobs around the cottage in exchange for reading lessons. Both felt a new purpose, and who knew what else might come of this relationship?

The wedding was to take place at St. Magnus on June twenty-fifth. A spacious venue was necessary because the guest list was going to be long. Everybody in Kirkwall was so happy for Ty, and they had quickly fallen in love with his bride-to-be, who would also be their school's new teacher. There would be fairies from far and wide in attendance, and of course Ty's friend, Edgar Degas, was invited. There was a brief discussion about where to hold the wedding feast, but in Ty's opinion there was only one place. Thistle Downe. As soon as they realized how important it was to him everyone readily agreed. The house was finally finished. In celebration, Lord and Lady Fleming presented Ty and Amelia with a beautiful heirloom silver tea service, which they proudly placed on the sideboard in their dining room.

One afternoon, Lord Fleming took Ty aside and suggested that perhaps the house was not quite finished. It was lacking a carriage house for the silver carriage that would belong to Amelia one day soon. Ty at first started to say that he hoped Lord and Lady Fleming would enjoy the carriage for years to come, but Lord Fleming held up a hand to stop him from speaking. "It is time for me to confide in you, Ty. There is something very important that you need to know. Here, come outside and sit with me for a moment in the carriage."

Ty nodded in assent, and they moved to the courtyard of the house. Once they had seated themselves inside the elegant coach, Lord Fleming indicated the oval mirror over the rear-facing passenger seat.

"Look into that mirror." Ty obeyed. At first, he saw nothing but his own reflection. When he blinked, he saw the hazy image of a girl troll, her face framed by a cloud of glossy black ringlets.

Suddenly, he felt a shock of recognition at the sight of her radiant smile. He rubbed his eyes and looked again. Although he had never seen her, he recognized her smile as exactly his own. "Is that my mother? It must be my mother! I have always wanted to see her! How is this possible?"

Lord Fleming smiled. "Well, Ty, this carriage is endowed with incredible supernatural powers. It can transport you into the future or into the past. As a student of history, you must have thought about long-ago events and wondered what led up to them or what it was like to witness them. This carriage makes it possible to answer your questions. For instance, you could go to America to experience the political climate that led to the revolution against England. You might attend the inauguration of their first President, George Washington. Or perhaps you might travel to Russia to visit the court of Catherine the Great at the beautiful Winter Palace in St. Petersburg. I once enjoyed that experience myself. Do you ever look at the moon and wonder whether anyone will ever reach it? This powerful carriage can take you far enough into the future to satisfy your curiosity."

He continued, "I know how greatly you have been affected by the absence of your mother in your life. Since your father's return, I understand you have learned a little more about her, but you never had a chance to see her. So, I arranged to have her appear in the carriage mirror. The good news is that soon, when Amelia inherits this coach, she will be able to time-travel and take you with her. You will be able to go into the past and spend time with your mother."

Ty sat quietly, absorbing this startling information. Then a memory struck him.

"Wait a minute, sir. When the carriage is preparing to travel in time, is it drawn by a winged white horse?" Startled, Lord Fleming asked how Ty could know such a thing.

"One night when Amelia was so ill, I was at the edge of your road keeping watch. I thought I saw your carriage harnessed to a winged white horse, but was sure that I must have dreamt it." "Yes," replied Lord Fleming. "When the carriage is preparing to travel in time, our Clydesdale assumes his true identity as Pegasus, the legendary winged horse. He can easily navigate the skyways at warp speed.

"On the occasion when you saw us, we were both in too much of a hurry. The horse showed himself prematurely and had to reverse his transformation. I had no idea that anyone had seen it happen. That was the night I took the carriage into the future to learn whether or not Amelia would survive her illness. Her mother and I could not stand the anxiety and strain any longer. Indeed, I did see her...and you.

"You must understand that *Tempus Fugit* members can observe past or future events, but they cannot try to change or influence the outcome. They can only adjust their own attitudes or convictions as a result of what they have seen. When I saw you in Amelia's future, I was upset, but I could do nothing to change the fact that you were there. Having to deal with that fact eventually changed me."

Lord Fleming stopped speaking. He and Ty sat companionably together, lost in their own thoughts.

Then, Lord Fleming resumed. "In your carriage house, you must build a tower to accommodate the very large crystal that charges the coach. It is the conduit between the universal force field and the receivers housed within the carriage that in turn communicate with Pegasus.

"The horse has been in my family for generations, giving wings to whatever conveyance was being used for travel. The silver carriage only goes back three generations, but the crystal has been in my family forever. Before the silver carriage it charged whatever the Traveler was driving at that time. We want Amelia to inherit the coach as soon as you have a place for it. I have told her this and she is eager and excited. She wants to take you to visit your mother at the earliest opportunity."

Ty didn't want to push his great good fortune by asking if his father could be included in such a trip as well. He would save that for a later day.

And, of course, he had the carpenters start construction of the carriage house the very next morning.

As a wedding gift for Amelia, Ty had a craftsman design and build a handsome grandfather clock with a brass pendulum and a rich, melodious chime. On its face appeared the Latin words, *horas non numero nisi serenas.* Translated, it meant, "I count only happy hours."

On June 24th, a sign went up over the door to the house. It read, "Thistle Downe 1862." Ty's heart nearly burst with pride, gratitude and anticipation. At noon the next day, St. Magnus was filled with wedding guests. On the groom's side were several hundred Orcadians, many friends from both Kirkwall and Stromness. Proudly Gareth, Mrs. Higbee, Miss McNamara, Corky and Ozzie sat in the front pew along with a very special guest, Edgar Degas, who had come all the way from Paris. On the bride's side were many fairies, all elegantly dressed and fluttering their wings constantly, causing a fragrant breeze in the great cathedral. Ty, dressed in a dark suit, his red hair combed as carefully as was possible, approached the chancel accompanied by his good friend, Mr. Higbee.

The ancient pipe organ began a processional, and Amelia, lovely in heirloom lace, came toward him on the arm of her father. Ty's merry eyes suddenly brimmed with tears of happiness. His life, which had started under such dismal circumstances, had come to include wonderful, loyal friends, an education, a successful business, and an unexpected reunion with his father. Now Amelia, who held the key to his heart, was only moments away from becoming his wife. He moved as if in a dream, taking her hand and resting it lightly on his arm.

Later, at Thistle Downe, there was a great celebration. Bagpipers lined the long drive and escorted the happy couple into their new home. Well-wishers crowded around them. The home welcomed their family and friends. Its windows glowed and its woodwork gleamed. Tables groaned with the weight of platters heaped full of tempting food, much of it prepared by the wedding guests themselves, according to custom. There were great platters of mutton, roast beef and smoked salmon and trays of cheddar cheese, traditional dumplings, shortbread and Orkney fudge. Of course there was plenty of sticky toffee pudding. Much later in the evening, the fireplace crackled and the smoke curled lazily from the chimney. Ty's friend, Edgar Degas, had brought with him two packages which, when opened, revealed portraits of both Amelia and Ty, who was overcome at the generosity of this young man. He immediately hung the portraits on either side of his prized fireplace for all to admire. He knew that this friendship would endure, and once again he caught his breath in amazement at his life. He silently thanked his mother for giving him her happy heart and wished that she were here to share his joy. He sent her a silent kiss that said, "I'll see you soon." He looked at his father with thankfulness that Gareth's life had been redeemed.

Placing his arm protectively around his bride, he saluted his new family and his old friends, his face transformed by his wonderful smile. He was ready to start his joyous new journey with Amelia, down the road to Happily Ever After.

The End

(or actually, just a new beginning!)

Epilogue

"Does it really exist?"

The story of Thistle Downe is a fairy tale. One of the most wonderful aspects of this fairy tale is that the troll, fairy, and human characters interact with each other without regard to their respective sizes. Their story takes place on the magical island of Mainland, Orkney, Scotland in the middle of the 19th Century. Even today, folktales about trolls and fairies abound in the culture of the island.

The question persists… could Thistle Downe possibly really exist? Is there really a miniature home built by a troll for himself and his fairy bride? It would be nearly impossible to find it because it is quite small, you realize. It has been told that a wren built its nest on the roof of the house, covering a goodly portion of it. It is highly likely that, by now, it is concealed by low-growing branches and undergrowth, which would make it almost impossible to find.

The fact is that it does exist as an actual testimony of love. It is the creation of Gary and Molly B. Whitney of Houston, TX. The original portion of the house, which he built from twigs he gathered from Hermann Park in Houston, was a Christmas gift to Gary's children. Louisiana and Alabama pinecones supplied material for the roof. In the early years it was a playhouse for the children's collection of trolls. Later, it served as a centerpiece for holiday celebrations complete with Halloween, Thanksgiving, and Christmas trolls.

Years later, Molly envisioned yet another role for this now abandoned playhouse. She imagined adding exterior facades, stained glass windows, interior and exterior lighting, hand-made furnishings, and most of all, an inspired story, true to the home's history. It is a love story about a troll who builds a life and a home for himself and his fairy bride...he names it "Thistle Downe."

Several years of additional construction ensued, inspired by the story unfolding in Molly's manuscript. Many of the items in the house are a part of her story, which evolved to include the time-traveling silver carriage and suggested a pre-quel and sequel. The home's additions include a living room, library, guest wing, and carriage house, surrounded by walls and terraces of stone.

We invite you to see Thistle Downe for yourself on our web-site. Here you will find photographs of the home under con-struction as well as the finished rooms and their occupants, a collection of over thirty Cicely Mary Barker flower fairies. Guests who visit are inspired and enchanted. The most com-mon comment they offer is, "Oh, I want to live in there!"

Meanwhile, let Thistle Downe exist in your heart happily ever after!

MBW & GSW

www.thistledownehouse.com

Sticky Toffee Pudding

This traditional Scottish dessert is best described as a dense date cake with an orange overtone, thoroughly saturated with a dark caramel sauce, served warm with whipped cream or crème fraiche topping.

Cake:

- Preheat oven to 350 degrees (Fahrenheit)
- Generously butter bottom and sides of 9" X 13" sheet baking pan.
- 1 cup pitted medjool dates, coarsely chopped
- ¾ cup water
- 1 cup plus 2 tablespoons all-purpose flour
- 1 teaspoon baking powder
- ¼ teaspoon baking soda
- pinch of salt
- ¾ cup light brown sugar
- 1 teaspoon pure vanilla extract
- 1 large egg
- 1 ½ tablespoon orange zest (grated orange peel)

Combine pitted dates and water in medium saucepan.

Cook until dates are softened or 15 minutes. Puree and allow to cool.

In large mixing bowl, beat brown sugar and butter until creamy. While beating, add vanilla, egg, orange zest, and date puree. Slowly, add the dry ingredients.

The resulting batter will be quite thick.

Pour into prepared baking pan, spreading till even. Bake for 40 minutes or until toothpick comes out dry. Turn onto cooling rack, removing from pan.

After cool, slice cake into two equally thick layers.

Toffee Sauce:

- 2 ½ cups heavy cream
- 1 cup sugar
- ½ cup light corn syrup
- 1 stick sweet unsalted butter

In heavy saucepan over medium heat, combine half of the heavy cream (1 ¼ cups) with the sugar, corn syrup, and butter. Cook, slow stirring continually until caramel forms and mixture turns to a dark golden color. This can take up to 40 minutes. Remove from heat, and SLOWLY add the remaining heavy cream, stirring continually. Return to heat just until sauce is smooth and thick.

While still warm, pour ⅓ of toffee sauce into bottom of sheet cake pan. Top with the bottom layer of the cake.

Pour another ⅓ of toffee sauce on top of that, followed by the top layer of the cake, and ending with the remaining ⅓ of the toffee sauce. Using a wooden skewer, repeatedly

Using a wooden skewer, repeatedly pierce holes in the cake from top to bottom, allowing the caramel to thoroughly saturate the cake. Place covered cake pan in warm oven for 30 minutes.

Serve individual portions in small bowls, topped with a dollop of unsweetened whipped cream or crème fraiche. Vanilla ice cream also works for a topping.

Enjoy!"

Tyson Kelly

Acknowledgments

Our thanks to so many people. To the editors and staff at Bright Sky Press, whose thoughtful guidance helped us to develop a much better story than the one we took to them. On the way we fell in love with our characters and came to wholeheartedly believe in our book. Thank you to friends and family who proofed the manuscript and made so many insightful suggestions and observations and to those who encouraged and supported us in countless other ways—grandsons Joe and Sam McKay, Klinka Lollar, Ken Boren, Ashley Everett, Valerie Sarver, Frank and Judy Douglas, the Bookends, Gay Estes, Mary Heartlein, and Lois Thomsen. We are grateful to Carol Coco Lee, who kept Gary's imaginative original tabletop twig house safe for a number of years and returned it to us when it had a new purpose in life. From it grew a beautiful art piece and the inspiration for this book.

Special thanks to Molly's ancestors, who inspired us to set this story in the Orkney Islands of Scotland, and to two current residents of this charming and mystical place. We have taken some liberties with the beautiful island of Mainland. Forgive us, Peter Leith and Patricia Leith Long.

Molly Boren Whitney & Gary Whitney